A Letter for Gigglepot

ambalika

First published in 2020 by

Becomeshakespeare.com

One Point Six Technologies Pvt. Ltd.
119-123, 1st floor, Building No. J2, Wadala East,
Wadala Truck Terminal, Mumbai, Maharashtra 400037, India
T: +91 8080226699

This book has been funded by WORDIT ART FUND
WORDIT ART FUND helps deserving
Authors publish their work
To apply for funding, please visit us at
becomeshakespeare.com

Copyright © 2020 by ambalika

©
ISBN-978-93-90266-63-0

DEDICATION

To my ex-students
(As I don't have an option)

For having loved me unconditionally
(As they didn't have an option)

Thankfully, this book is not about you or me.

But supposing you start reading it and you are reminded of yourself or me or someone you know, then, well, may be, perhaps, as a matter of fact…uh-huh… well, then my bad.

Proceeds from this book will be invested in wildlife conservation activities in Assam and North East, with a special focus on saving the one-horned rhino.

ACKNOWLEDGMENT

Special thanks to Mr. Jahnu Barua, the renowned Assamese film maker who quickly agreed to read this manuscript and suggest improvements as well, while generously peppering encouragements all along. Given that I was- still am- a nobody, this meant (then) - still does- a lot. The confidence and joy I feel as I think about it, is indescribable. I am grateful to him for his time and valuable suggestions.

CONTENTS

1	The Letter	11
2	Shadow of Death	18
3	Being Fired	21
4	The Way Home	27
5	College!	29
6	The Gang	35
7	Imranpur	40
8	The Ride to Imranpur	43
9	First Impressions	48
10	The Blessed of Imranpur	50
11	A New Beginning	54
12	At the College	62
13	The Start of Something New	67
14	Next Door Neighbours	71

15   Sunday   77

16   Getting Started   84

17   Opening Googly   89

18   Insecure Security   95

19   One Hell of Progress   100

20   The Inspector   104

21   When Thoughts Made the Man   109

22   Tuesday   113

23   A Play of Time   115

24   Maharani Theatres   117

25   Me   122

26   Saikia's Day in the Sun   128

27   The Call   130

28   The Action Plan   133

29   Saikia's Second Call   136

30   A Teacher's Suspicions   141

31   Sista Code   145

32	Saikia's Grandfather	148
33	Newspapers In Action	151
34	Our Neighbour At War	159
35	The Truth	163
36	Dinesh Barua	171
37	Koka Again	173
38	Dinesh Barua Again	176
39	Aunt Sarah's Truth	179
40	The Hospital	186
41	My Truth	189
42	Busted!	194
43	Calling the Bluff	205
44	The End of Beginning	209
45	Carrying On	213

1 THE LETTER

It came on a Sunday afternoon. The call, that is. From Aunt Sarah. She had called to inform me about the passing away of an uncle. I had no recollection of who this gentleman was. I told her so. She agreed saying that after all, he was a little distant in the scheme of relations. However, she went on, he had left behind a letter for me.

Now, that was rather incredible.

For, having been unaware of his existence, I never had the chance to partake of any interactions with him. So, I could only guess and ponder over the fanciful thoughts that must have come around in making him write a letter to me in the twilight of his life. Perhaps he had a secret which he needed to get off his conscience, so he could go in peace? After all, it is in this stage of life, that the good and the sensible look back at the life that they have lived wondering if they had done it all right. That upon their departure, they would not be causing unwanted and untold grief, sadness, anger and a sense of vengeance.

A joke.

I considered the angle.

'You go ahead and read it, Auntie.'

I could hear deep grunts of disagreement being made by Aunt at the suggestion. Okay, so it's serious, I told myself. Giving it a quick thought, I asked her if I needed to come to collect the letter. After all, he was my father's lost-somewhere-long-in-the-lines cousin. It felt the right thing to do. But she said there was no need for that. She would mail it to me, instead.

Thus it was that, the following weekend, I found myself in possession of a letter that contained within it, another letter. This first letter, which was written by my uncle, told me that the letter enclosed was of utmost importance and that once I read it my life would change forever. He regretted his inability to share this with me earlier but was sure I would understand why. That he had been bound by his word – to whom he would not specify. So, I was to not take it personally and forgive him for it, as this was how it had all been planned out. He ended it by wishing me the very best in life.

It was one of the most straight forward writing I had read in recent times. But though I appreciated his directness, I felt a little uncertain about what I was going to find inside the second letter. However, given the monotonous life that I was living, this was a welcome change. The prospect excited me. I wanted to read the letter instantly, rather than continue playing the 'letter points to letter' game. It was therefore that, with a high dose of eagerness, I finally opened the actual letter.

I read it. Sure, it read well. It was a letter by my father to me. He too, had written to me in his last hours. This desire of elderly gentlemen to write to me just as they were departing from life felt very spooky. But perhaps that in itself might have been the reason why I was convinced that the letter was going to offer some exciting news. Though after reading it the first time I could not figure out what exactly was it. I had to read the letter another half a dozen times to get what it was trying to convey.

At the end, I got it.

I understood, from the correspondence, that the man, whom I had been calling father all along till now, was not my Father. He was just my 'father'. I had another Father, an original one who went by the name of 'Bharadwaj'. The letter did not throw any light on what had become of my Father or who he was likely to be. All it said in this aspect was that he had disappeared at some 'Lake of No Return' during a war on the state border. That sounded like some kind of a charm. The letter spoke nothing more on this-what this lake was -did it exist at all or was it some code word-, why did he get attracted to it, whether he was alone or was there a group of men along with him, where did this happen, how did the 'lake' cause 'no return' and details like that.

Once the initial excitement passed over, it occurred to me that I was holding on to a rather useless piece of information. My stand-in father was long dead and my original father was not likely to be alive and kicking either. My mother continued to be my mother though, that was of little help as she had passed away a month before my stand-in father's death.

So why bother?

It was then that realizations started dawning on me. It began with my existing social identity of being the offspring of a 'firang' father and 'desi' mother getting shattered. Though I must admit that, in the past, I myself did have some suspicion on this occasionally. My genetic make-up was the first pointer. For, it had not passed my notice that somehow I didn't seem to have any 'firangi' features. But a confirmation right then, on this, came as a shaker. I was shaken to the core. 'Who Am I?' was no longer a philosophical question for me. It had become a matter of existential crisis.

I had always been Ashima B. Brendon, daughter of Mr. James Brendon who in turn was the older son of Jane and Chris Brendon who had travelled all the way from Tilbury in England by ship through Gibraltar, Marseilles, Port Said before reaching Mumbai and then took the train to Calcutta and later Jorhat, to take up the superintendence of the Duroni Tea Estate. While they left for their home when their term ended, they let James and his sister Sarah stay behind.

James, because he had taken up the job at the same estate and Sarah because she was now married here to a Mr. Phukan.

Of the unexpanded 'B' in my name, I did not pay much attention to.

I figured that it must have something to do with my mother's maiden surname. Possibly one of those, which are long and have an unusual pronunciation—something like Bisheshwarnathorkanya.

Bisheshwarnathorkanya.

Bisheshwar Nath's daughter, that is. That would have been just as well had I been kidding, but not in reality-which is why it was best left unexpanded. It had never struck me that I should make an enquiry to find out if it was actually the case. Life had gone on, without complications and I did not see any reason why I should not let it be that way.

That it stood for Bharadwaj came as quite a stunner. Firstly, because it was shorter than Bisheshwarnathorkanya, one thing that I had not expected. Secondly, it sounded very modern and a cool surname to have as against Bisheshwarnathorkanya which casts out images of long haired, lean thin priests who do nothing but chant prayers all day and hold in contempt anything that's fun and different. And lastly, because I learnt of it despite having absolutely no inclination of ever expecting to uncover this mystery.

But now that I had been stunned, I could feel a Brendon vs Bharadwaj war beginning to rage within me.

My current paternal side brought me up. Though I never did meet the grandparents; for all that boat journey scared my mother. We did write letters to each other and were on very good terms. The maternal side however, had always been courteous, in a cold sort of way. In fact, it would not be totally wrong to say that when people weren't looking, they openly disowned me by not paying any attention and tolerating me only on social occasions. Guess the 'desi-videsi' union was too scandalous for the times.

But right then, *I* was feeling scandalized at having discovered an 'original' paternal side to my existence.

I had no clue what I had to be now- a Brendon or a Bharadwaj. Even if I didn't want to make up my mind, I had to for the sake of society. Application forms always ask for a father's name and I had two. I had been walking around with both of my dads' names and never had felt so bugged. Maybe, because, now I had to choose one. Which dad? - was the question.

I must say, I never felt so surprised by life and the questions it throws, ever before. I was in a state of grave despair that I did not like. I tried getting out of it by trying to focus on something else. But it was very difficult. I felt being held back by something, someone. And it was not long before I realized that, this, was the doing of The Lake of No Return; it was responsible for my double mindedness.

Where was this? Why did my father have to go there? Not that men have not been known to disappear in lakes. But then water bodies have been known to exist for better and more productive reasons. What had this one done to my father and the other men who were with him, if any? The mystery had indeed caught my imagination.

Not only that, it also brought about a change in my lifestyle. No longer did I now want to spend my Saturday afternoons watching movies or sleeping away. Instead, I began to prefer spending them pursuing leads on this lake and the case of the unknown father. It was not an easy job since I had very little information to start with. All I knew was that a certain Mr. Bharadwaj had gone missing during a war in the border in a lake and because of this I had a substitute dad who was a man of foreign origin. I knew this was going to be a most frustrating search. But I had to demystify this for my own sake.

My sudden loss of identity called for this.

I wished I was back at the Burra Bungalow at the Duroni Tea Estate. Back in that time when I was somewhere between crawling on all fours and managing to tug along on my feet as I clung on to my two older cousins Eddie and Amy, Aunt Sarah's children. There was no need to bother with who was who or who wasn't, then. This latter point being majorly emphasized by the absence of Aunt's husband who never seemed to be bothered about us.

We, too, somehow never got to call him *Uncle*. For us he was always Aunt's *husband*. When we grew older, we came to know that, that was because he had passed away tragically- shot by insurgents along with his father when returning from Guwahati by car. Eddie, being the eldest of us, had a faint recollection of the funeral but was not sure. Amy had no memory while I wasn't even thought of at that time. So the tragic-ness was lost on us.

Despite this background, they were fun times. We were either partying or playing. And I was smart at both.

Once, a certain Mr. Cooper had come visiting us. He was another of those expat progenies who had been born and bred in the garden of tea and had decided to keep up the tradition. Having had considerable success at this, he believed himself to be possessing of that niche quality of parenting skills required to nurture children born into a cross of cultures. It was with this faith that he decided to befriend me. Making me sit on his lap, he entertained me in his heavy British accent with the Assamezised -Hindi version of the un-funnily fateful tale of the Humpty Dumpty. Sang he:

Humpty Dumpty upar mein boitha,

Humpty Dumpty gir giya phut!

Sara raja ka manos aur rajah ka ghora,

Humpty Dumpty ko kabhi nahi jora!

When he had finished, I jumped off his lap and unfurling the frills of my dainty little frock, recited the adventure of a 'Little Miss Muffet' who 'sat on a tuffet, eating her curds and whey' in chaste English pronunciation.

I was *that* smart.

But now, with that letter in hand, I didn't feel anything like that. I was instead reminded of that big, bulky, bad, bullying boy at school who used to harass me with questions like why wasn't my skin white; why weren't my eyes blue, why wasn't I blonde haired, if my father was indeed an Englishman.

What was he trying to mean? That I was one of those coffee coloured products of Englishmen who had '*gone native*' on the tea estates that were looked down upon by the memsahibs?

I would hide in a lonely corner of the playground and cry till my eyes ran dry.

Yes, I am coffee coloured. But no, I am not one of those children looked down upon and certainly not by the memsahibs on the estate. And no, my father had not *gone native*. His sister, my beloved Aunt Sarah, had fixed his marriage to my mother. In an age where young English chaps freshly landed at tea estates were frequently getting serious about many a local girl, this was a significant departure. But despite being too little to understand what this significant departure signified, I fully used it for my defence.

But what would that big, bulky, bad, bully understand of all these? And yet, after all these years, suddenly his questions seemed real.

2 SHADOW OF DEATH

Meanwhile, at a certain distance away, on the fifth floor of the Administrative Block, West Wing, the door stood slightly ajar. Beyond it lay a collection of water tanks arranged in a haphazard fashion and somewhere in the midst of these sat a huddled figure. But on this side of the door, there was nothing to betray that human presence. The only evidence of life was the swaying of the door, without any pace, whenever the wind blew with a little vengeance. Otherwise, silence and arrogance filled the space.

That, however, was not the way things were laid out for that human presence on the other side of the door. Total mayhem and severe unrest was brewing in its heart and soul so much so that it stood up, and walking to the nearest edge of the terrace, contemplated jumping off. The spot seemed just right. Not only would no one see, no one would even come to know about it until quite sometime. A time sufficient to have entered after-life by then.

A human presence can be a weird entity. Much like a door that can either open itself revealing the endless possibilities which lay ahead of it or it can stay shut leaving it to the wit and imagination of everyone around to guess and gauge what it may be hiding from them.

What a weird entity the human presence can be, indeed! Either it can choose to melt into its surroundings or it can ignore it as if it never existed in the first place.

'That should be easy enough', there came a thought as the left leg went off the ground and anticipated a push from the right leg. Now, that set the ground for a debate between the progressive and digressive thinking.

'Are you sure?'

'What do you mean?'

'Well, easy ones are easily the most difficult.'

'What?'

'Oh, you haven't heard?'

'Heard what?'

'Fundamental law of nature.'

'What's that?'

'What I just told you.'

'Nonsense.'

'It's true.'

'Shut up.'

The leg came back to its original position of rest on the ground. Doubt seemed to have finally found a foothold.

'But I've had it!!!', screamed the voice of the soul.

'Pax, now!' Commanded the brain. 'And think.' So the brain reasoned.

One, what if death wasn't instant?

Gosh! It would be terrible to die a little at a time, over a period of time.

Two, what if Attempted Death instead led to Attainment of a Vegetative State?

O Blimey, how utterly disgusting!

Three, what if no death happened at all?

Enough!!!

This whole dialogue process turned out to be more torturous than committing the act of self inflicted death itself. Suddenly, trying to die lost all its charm and therefore no longer appeared as an attractive option.

Not left with a suitable alternative, Antony Ashoke Baruah climbed down all five flights of stairs on the West Wing of the Administrative Block and walking straight towards classroom number 5 on the East Wing of Education Block joined his fellow classmates for another session on Thermodynamics, at the prestigious Institute for Technical Education, Imranpur.

Life, as people say, has its own ways. No arguing that.

3 BEING FIRED

Given all that exotic and adventurous upbringing that I had, my current lifestyle was confirmedly a lame and tame one. It was the all predictable world of the ubiquitous 'IT professional'- so revered, so sought after, that the side effects which it breeds is very often overlooked or accepted as a 'price worth paying' for being part of an 'elite' brand. All that, on the face of it, though.

The reality, when put in words, is neither revered nor sought after-able.

I have seen that reaction many times. The 'So, what's it like?' is often asked with an extra dose of enthusiasm only to be scrummed off by my reply- 'Up in the morning, then to office and back'. Not to be undone, a more hopeful 'What about weekends?' is put. This one gets a mono worded reply- 'Sleep', which single handedly dashes any further desires on finding out anything more.

Honestly, what is so exciting about sitting in an air conditioned cubicle in an exotically designed office spread over acres, for beyond the mandatory eight point five hours, writing computer codes and speaking in altered accents over telephonic status calls with unseen clients who sit in North America or Europe or APAC or EMEA, as they are popularly referred to by the marketing guys and the management?

Perhaps it's the lure of the IT world that comes in the form of Onsite in a foreign land or the belief that we are adding value to 'our customers' by helping them understand 'their customers'. Either ways, sorry, I don't have time for such a roundabout way of getting things done.

Just like I have little acceptance of having my life reduced to that of a sleeping bag that wakes up only towards the evening of the weekend and opts to eat from the street side vendor because cooking or going to a more decent eatery is hard work.

Come on, even the part time maid seems to have a more fulfilling and exciting life!

Well, tea estates are not the breeding grounds for 'techies'.

I grew up in the company of tamed wilderness. There were monkeys to chase after, snakes to be chased by, trees to climb, fruits to pluck, ponds to swim across or fish in, which is the great Assamese national time-pass. Then, there were the surrounds of hills and mountains. My heart lay in trekking through them to decode the secrets that they held up. That was the kind of Analyst and Code Breaker I had dreamt of being. I did not want to leave behind the life on the estate.

But daddy had said, no.

In one of his weekly letters to me when I was at the boarding school, he wrote that 'The Brendons should diversify' and that they need 'to be flexible and look at opportunities for new learning.'

The tone was in stark contrast to the ones I had been receiving until then, when he would begin with a jolly 'Hi Gigglepot!' and enquire what new tricks I had learnt. No trace of any dynastic ambitions or plans there. I suspected that it must have come from one of those management journals that he had recently started subscribing to, which I knew he was reading with devotion.

I never liked any of those and so tried talking him out of it. I mentioned that climbing mountains was also part of the diversification process. But when I received a particularly insistent letter saying 'Enough of tea brewing', I understood that he was beyond me.

And so it came about that I ended up being the first of 'The Brendons' to 'diversify' from 'tea brewing' by taking up engineering and then stepping into the world of IT at the Electronics City Phase I in Bengaluru. A life event that ensured all of the mountain climbing went up the clouds.

But now that I had discovered, I was not one of 'The Brendons', I was convinced that I was cheating myself by being in the job. I had got into it under, what I now came to regard as, false guidance from persons falsely related to me and so firmly believed that this falsity should end.

In simple words, I reasoned that this was ground enough to quit what I was doing and take to what I had always wanted to do. Convinced of my own thoughts, I made up my mind. However, when I called up my Aunt Sarah to tell her of my plan, it occurred to me that something about it was not correct. As of then, I had not even told her of what that letter was all about. But knowing it myself, my inner voice whispered that, perhaps, I would be belittling the goodwill of 'The Brendons', by doing so.

I ended up mentioning nothing on the matter to her. Fate, however, had heard of my desires through its large, long ears and decided to take some action on it.

A few days later, one morning at the office, providence weaved a set of events as only it could. The direct result of which was something that could not be written in a resume'.

Like the reason for leaving a previous job. On the face of it, this is a saver. One is saved the embarrassing task of putting to words, quite unnecessarily, the ordeals that are best forgotten. But below that face, it remains the single fact that can make or break further career aspirations during the interview for the next job. I know this because I faced it and trust me, it is not at all a pleasant situation to be in. To put it in simple words, this is what happened- I was fired.

I was just three months into the job and it was my first. But I am not going to defend myself. Many theories on my unceremonious dismissal did the rounds and a good percentage of them are pretty derogatory in nature. Now, I don't want to suggest that Dismissal Theories are meant to give image makeovers. I merely want to state that if anyone must know why I was fired, they may as well hear it from the horse's mouth, which happens to be my own mouth, in this case.

And it is this- I was caught entertaining myself as I read my friends' status updates on a social networking site when I should have been actively pursuing 'bugs' on a web application under development. I did this in the presence of my manager who, in turn was in the presence of Our Esteemed Client.

I had committed an unpardonable act.

It amounted to violation of both Company Internet Usage Policy as well as the HR Policy. And, to cut a long story short, I underwent the Exit Procedure.

'Would you like to say something?'

'No.'

This was not a court case and I was not defending myself- there was no need for it. So why they even bothered with this question, I did not understand. Perhaps they wanted me to apologize. But to be honest, I did not get this point either.

My only regret was that at the time of being caught I was not logged on to WarVeterans.com or FindingGraves.com. That way at least, I would have not lost valuable time that could have been spent gathering information. Because by then, not only had the mysterious 'Lake of No Return' cast its spell on me but also I was beginning to admittedly get a little more curious of the whereabouts of my supposedly 'original father'.

First of all, was that letter even true?

What if it was someone with the intention of creating a family feud and could not be stopped who had written this, imitating the handwriting?

I put this question to my Aunt after I told her about the letter rather dispassionately and in a concise manner that didn't go beyond, 'old man wrote to say I am not of the family.' Her immediate reaction was an 'Oh!' uttered in shock that was followed by a more controlled 'hmm'. When I had asked her if it was so, she responded by asking me if I had ever felt so. I never had. 'So then why are you even asking it?' She rebuked me mildly.

'But then why did he write it?'

'I don't know.'

She sounded angry by now. I then put my theory to her. Aunt agreed that indeed such people existed in this world but even if they had worked that way in this case, they shouldn't be paid any attention to.

'I just hope this doesn't change things the way they are.'

'Of course, auntie! I don't see a reason too!'

So that was it. Between us, this matter was sorted.

But what I didn't feel sorted was, why was that letter even written in the first place. Forced or self motivated, James Brendon did write it. My eyes were telling me that. And I increasingly had a desire to know –why. Surely, there couldn't be smoke without fire.

I also knew that if I had to find the answer to this question, then it was going to come from my other father. So I set to work, reading and hunting for any piece of information that I could find.

I carried this to my office too, where, bored by work, I would take to searching for that lake and clues for inspiring disappearances from around it. Now, that was definitely something substantially irritating- looking up the dead or searching lost people now dead *is.* Especially from the unimaginative and mechanical viewpoint of the management who could very well justify my firing even over this rather than harping over my tendency to social network at work.

But I am not the one to complain and so, most courteously, accepted the route out. This was another first for me, a former member of 'The Brendons'. When I called up Aunt Sarah to tell her about it, she said that she had seen this coming. A most helpful response for me since I was spared of giving out the details. I didn't bother her with how she foresaw this. After all, like me, she too needed privacy with her secrets.

4 THE WAY HOME

I have a deep sense of trust towards my fascinations. In fact, one could say that I feel an obligation towards fulfilling them. Most certainly and as recently, my virtual pursuance of the Lake of No return has been a reflection of this. But I have also had another one of them. It is the fascination with *the river*.

I woke up with a jolt. I opened my eyes and felt a little surprised at being on a train. Had I not been lying on a *dhongi*, that small little boat, and cruising silently along a river and then got sucked into a whirlpool?

Well, having woken up pretty safe and sound on the seat of the train, it definitely seemed otherwise. Perhaps I had foreseen something?

I drew aside the curtains of my seat window and looked out. We were chugging and gliding along, giving out the engine horn occasionally. It was still daylight. We were going past ponds, cattle and farmers and as far as I could see, the fields were stretching quite far off as if to meet the horizon. No chance of a river. I smiled at myself. Rather, at my dream. It seemed like that was all I was left with.

Perhaps it is a fascination that has been inherited. But then who am I to discuss inheritance? I, who know not of my own parentage!

I was first introduced to this river as a child, up in the arms of my daddy. Wherever we went by train, we had to cross 'The Bridge'. It was inevitable whether going in or coming out of Guwahati. 'The Bridge', with the river below and the road above it, held its own charm. We knew that we were approaching it, when the train began to move along letting the tracks go lower than the road, gradually. That being the first indication of the approach. Standing by the door of the coach, he would hold me up to let me get the full view of the river, which would only be restricted by the steel ridges of the bridge.

I remember being taken in by the enormity of the river. A river that wide? I was alarmed. My alarmed mumbles gave way to silence, initially, because of the scare it gave me but later, out of respectful appreciation that I began to feel regarding its mightiness. That was how I had come to think of 'The River.'

Being too young for any distinct and sensible uttering, I would show my fascination by waving my arms wide and babbling, 'Blummpurra! Blummpurra!', almost as a chant. The name of the bridge, I didn't even bother with. Much wiser now, I knew what I saw and I knew what it was. Couple of hours later, when the train slowed down, gently parting ways from the road, allowing the road to go over the train, I knew that we were entering the Saraighat Bridge.

I put aside the refreshments tray that the pantry service boy had delivered sometime back and made my way to the door of the coach. There wasn't anyone on the corridor. Nor near the doors. From the change in the sounds that the wheels were making, I knew we had entered the bridge.

I jerked the door open and putting my hands over the hand rail on either side of the door, leaned forward; totally enjoying the thrill of what my eyes showed me- the might of the majestic Brahmaputra. Along the banks were a couple of *dhongis* cruising while the whirlpools were only in the middle of the river, quite a distance from them. Ahead, lay the tracks leading to the station, running past the Indian Institute of Technology and the gas cracker plant. I was home.

5 COLLEGE!

'I've told you many times, that's dangerous,' admonished Aunt Sarah as I gleefully narrated how thrilling it was to be over the river, like the way I did. Normally she was accompanied by Eddie or Amy or both when she said this and so I had my cousins' support, meaning she lost clearly three to one. But now Eddie was in Australia doing his Masters while Amy was studying in Delhi. So at this one-to-one, there was bound to be some stalemate, until one of us gave away. I was sure it wouldn't be me. At least, not *so* soon.

'*Edin beyake maar khabi*', she cautioned me about getting beaten one day, in halting Assamese. It had me stopped, not because the threat worked its effect on me but that it once again surprised me of two things about her. One, that she was indeed an English woman, but one who was dressed up in *mekhela-chador* and who cooked the tastiest *masor-tenga*, fish in sweet and sour sauce. And second, her lack of improvement with vocabulary or language fluency, despite the years spent living here with the Assamese people.

It was the same dialogue every time- 'One day you will get badly beaten'- from my childhood till now. After all these years, she could have at least got further by saying who would be doing the beating and how.

But then, I myself fared only slightly better. Framing my thoughts first in English and then doing a word by word translation to Assamese, had in the past, landed me at the wrong destination and made me pay wrong amount of money to the wrong people for the wrong stuff. It was just one of the many things that had happened.

'But Auntie, I was just viewing the river!' I got back with my reasoning. It didn't help. She began to speak of the things that were likely to happen to me in the event of my 'viewing' going wrong. The most notable one being- getting swallowed by the whirlpools that belie the silent demeanor of the river. I had heard that many times in the past and now again, of how two boys, from the office of where a neighbour worked, had gone to the river for 'just a dip' and never returned till date. Apparently the river had carried them away.

'That is what your 'viewing' will get you' she concluded.

'But auntie, I owe it respect', reminding her that it was owing to this river that I had become the Geography Star at school. In an otherwise drab class where neither the teacher nor the students had found the topic- Rivers of India- interesting, I livened up matters by not only telling them that the Brahmaputra had fifty eight tributaries but named all of them as well! I felt that this was a fairly good rebuttal. However, she cut me short with a 'the river doesn't understand such things'.

Anyway, the deed was done with and all had ended well. There was no need for further discussion. Thankfully, Aunt also agreed on this. Promptly handing me a towel, she conveyed this and added, 'Now get ready. I will drive you to the college.'

'*Col-lege?* '

'Yes.'

'Why?'

'You can teach there.'

'I can WHAT???'

I looked at her with a distasteful look which did not improve when she specified that it was an engineering college. In fact, I groaned. But she continued telling me how it was destined to become a bright and shining jewel among the academic centers of the country very soon in the future.

Going by her talk, it appeared that this college was everywhere- from newspapers to TV channels; from hoardings to the FM channels; ensuring that if not anything more, it was at least the talk of the town. To me it appeared as a rather gutsy college. I was beginning to wonder what the catch was when I heard Aunt wrap up her speech saying 'Imranpur'.

'What was that?' I jumped at the word.

'I said Imranpur. The college is based out of Imranpur.'

'*Imranpur*?'

There it was. I had caught it.

For, Imranpur is a village. And as far as I knew, the government was carrying out some work on primary education for children in the villages, not a mission of technical education for the late teens. Whatever was this college doing there?

Though no flourishing scholar myself, I was unable to warm up to the promise that this college showed. I mean, for all my academic short comings, I cannot be swept off my feet by an institution that shows up as a Tickr tape on TV channels and advertises itself between film songs on FM channels. Even if they were talking about 100% placements, success of students in the Graduate Aptitude Test for Engineers, developing robotic arms in their labs or made the offer of providing certifications in the latest technology.

I had formed my own ideas on this one. But Aunt had read in the papers that despite these lean beginnings, it was one of the foremost colleges that parents sought for their children in recent times. Obviously, that meant, it had the potential to make it big. So I could try. And since I did not have anything better to do, she thought I *should* give it a try. I hadn't expected this. It was not the kind of welcome I wanted or even remotely expected. 'Look around and if you like it, the principal will interview you and finalize the matter.'

Interview?

'But auntie-'

'No but-ting. You have been but-ting since the time you arrived.'

'I have not prepared for the interview,' I announced.

'Fat help your preparations have done', she said going on to remind that apart from the achievement in the geography class, I had nothing scholarly to show. So, I might as well go, see, chat and fix up things. Besides, she said, I had my 'work experience' to talk of.

Indeed.

I would, of course, not deny that I had worked hard enough to be at work and was being paid handsomely. Though, like many of my peers, I too wanted something better. If it was going to come about with the loss of a job, then so be it. I had lost no time in writing myself a profile on latestjobs.com and waited with bated expectations. What followed was a series of snowballing interviews. None however, led to anything worthwhile.

So rather than harping on my lack of preparation, which I knew was only a last ditch attempt to find an excuse to delay possible employment and enjoy a little vacation, I agreed to give the college a try. It did not sound that bad, even though it was wide away from the plan I had for myself, which mainly consisted of climbing mountains. Of course, I would do it for a cause, much like people ran marathons for a cause. I was sure that had I mentioned this to daddy Brendon, he would have approved of it since the idea had its similarity with Corporate Houses running and funding marathons and I myself was part of one. It would have fetched me another of his 'Hi Gigglepot, NOW you make me proud of you!' Unfortunately, it had not come to that.

Now, given that I had nothing to finance that plan or even remotely go about it, taking up this job made sense- if I could get it, that is. It also came with the promise of furnished quarters, which actually did mean a lot. At least, in terms of saving on the rent. Suddenly, the opportunity felt quite interesting.

It was in this interview that I shortly found myself in.

'Why do you want to make this switch of professions?', asked the gentleman sitting across the table after he quickly reviewed my CV, adjusting his glasses as he spoke.

To be challenged with such questions in the air conditioned interiors of a plush room felt a little odd. But I reminded myself that I was sitting in the presence of the Head of the Institute of Technical Education who held this job precisely to ask such questions and figure out the best fit on who could handle the prospective teaching assignment.

'I have academic interests.' I replied confident that this made me sound intellectual.

'In what?'

'In academics, naturally.'

'Excellent. Now, my question is – *What kind?*'

I had not foreseen this possibility of inquisitiveness in the interviewer while preparing myself for the interview during the drive to Imranpur. I mumbled something that was broadly peppered with the words- 'industry…limitation…academics…research' and then added a dollop of optimism with the statement, 'I want to learn and share my knowledge'. I had read in the 'Success tips' section of the highly reliable latestjobs.com that this is a 'deal clincher' statement to make. Potential employers normally fall for it even if there is gross lack of intent.

'Right.'

'Yes, sir.'

'You may wait outside. The Superintendent will speak to you.'

'Yes, sir.'

I thanked him and walked out of the room as politely as I could. To be in the corridor of the powers that be certainly could be a rattling experience. And at the corridor of the third floor, West Wing, Administrative Block, it felt exactly like that, making me wonder where my life was heading. Once outside, I sauntered around trying to fill time reading random notices on the Bulletin Board and trying to take a peek inside the Dr. B. N Saikia lab where a few students seemed to be busy in a discussion with their teacher.

Noticing a seemingly never ending flight of wide stairs, I followed it up and reached the library where large empty shelves greeted me. In a corner were box loads of books that were yet to be opened, catalogued and then set on the shelves ready for circulation. I walked up and down the long hall taking in the smell of the freshly painted walls and then went out, noticing that opposite to it was the Electronics lab.

Finding nothing more interesting to do or look, I went back to the Bulletin Board area and continued my wait. I stood leaning forward, my elbows resting on the low walls that looked into the quadrangle, staring at the construction work when a middle aged woman came up to me.

'Ashima B. Brendon?'

'Yes!'

She handed me an envelope giving me a half hearted scrutinizing look and then went off without another word. I opened the envelope and read the contents of the letter inside. The Principal of the Institute of Technical Education, Imranpur had appointed me as an Assistant Professor in the Department of Electronics & Communication Engineering.

6 THE GANG

They were four of them.

One of them was the victim. He was dressed in a red striped tee shirt and black checkered shorts with matching red and black floaters. Tall, thin and large eyed, he was downcast. The other three were, of course, the victimizers. They looked the part and seemed quite happy about it too.

Boy Number One- BoNO- had spiked hair and a tattoo twirling up his arm. Standing with his hands in the front pockets of his shorts, he certainly didn't seem to mind interrogation by the authority. Yet, he had an air of disinterest about him.

Boy Number Two- BoNuT- was chubby cheeked and with mild cherubic features. To the fleeting eye, he resembled 'Yours Innocently'. The fixed eye of course saw beyond this. Standing with his hands held in front of him, BoNuT understood the gravity of the situation but did not want to participate in its resolution.

Boy Number Three-BoNTree- was of a well built physique. As he stood with his arms folded in front of the authority, he certainly looked like he meant business. He must have actually meant business while violating the hostel rules as well. And right then, he looked equally well meaning too.

'What were you doing, huh? Tell me,' demanded the high pitched shrill voice embodied in flesh and blood as Minal Borthakur, In Charge of Hostel Operations at the Institute of Technical Education, Imranpur- IoTE to the rest of the world- pronounced and majorly written as 'Ayote', with the students taking pride in calling themselves- Ayotics.

'Nothing', replied BoNO.

'Uh-ho! Then why has this boy complained?' She asked pointing at the Red & Black victim. BoNO admitted he was clueless on this.

'And what have you to say on this?' She asked the other two.

'Yes, ma'am.' BoNuT responded as if coming out of a deep slumber.

'Ma'am', said BoNTree, meaning every syllable of it.

'Yes??', asked Minal feeling that something more was going to be shared. But apart from a sigh escaping from R&B, nothing else was uttered. The last thing they remembered was that they were in the Common Room to watch the TV.

'I was watching the documentary on Club 27', volunteered BoNO.

'I went there to watch Who Wants to Be the Next F1 Driver', started BoNuT.

'And I wanted to watch Snakes on The Animal Channel', said the 'Bo' who meant it all.

'What?' Asked Minal Ma'am.

'Yes ma'am!' They replied in chorus.

'That led to arguments, ma'am' offered BoNO.

'So we took off the TV card ma'am', informed BoNuT.

'So there was equality because none of us were watching it, ma'am', an unusual champion of equality in BoNTree spoke.

'WHAT? You… took… off… the…card???', lashed out Minal. Clearly, she hadn't expected this. Though, having being two years into the job and burnt her fingers dealing with mischief makers of the supreme order, she should have naturally guessed it.

'Yes', confirmed BoNuT

'How could you!'

'But it's safe with us, ma'am', BoNO offered some consolation.

'Don't talk to me like that!' She fired the words at him. 'I will let the Dean deal with that'

'Then what are we here for, ma'am?', asked BoNuT.

'Like you don't know!'

The Bo gang professed their ignorance on the matter and looked at R&B for help, with a 'Did-we-do-anything-to-you' look on their faces. Minal squirmed. She had to agree that there was something admittedly genuine about the boys' lost looks. But she was equally determined that they wouldn't have it easy with her.

'Six people saw the three of you barge into this fellow's room in the middle of the night and not come out until three hours later and you are asking me 'What are we here for, ma'am?' How dare you!' Minal ma'am said it all at one go. For someone in her capacity, containing indiscipline for too long didn't do any good.

'Oh, that!' BoNuT heaved a sigh of relief. 'We went in for a little chit chat.'

'Oh, hear, hear. What were you doing all day? No time to 'chit chat' then? Why at night?' She was running short of breath now.

'How can we talk to our juniors when we are attending classes ma'am?' BoNTree spoke. 'Aha! Don't I know that none of you attended any of the classes yesterday?' She would let the Dean deal with that, of course. 'But it is my business to know what business you had in his room at night.' Minal knew how to dig beyond perfectly well presented reasons.

'They were ragging me, ma'am!', cried R&B for the first time as he spoke for the first time.

'It's not true!', defended BoNuT. 'We only asked him to sing.'

'They said I sing like a horse chattering its teeth in the cold.'

Nobody defended this one. Not even Minal Ma'am. Probably, R&B's whining voice convinced her. So he continued. 'Then they made me imitate a monkey chattering its teeth in the cold.' Going by his narration, the 'Bo'ys had got him started on a mimicking spree.

'Actually ma'am, we wanted to audition for a new voice for the band.'

'In the middle of the night?'

'Ma'am, we had clas…'

'Nonsense!'

Like she didn't know what the nocturnal visit meant. She was also quite clear that this band business had to end. The last time this band played, it had led to a fight with the local DJ. Of course, she had not dealt with that. She had left it to the newly appointed Dean who made short work of it by suggesting that the Head look into it since he neither knew the students nor the DJ nor the context that demanded the music and the subsequent fight.

But for now, Minal gave one doze of counseling on Hostel Etiquettes and sent back all the four boarders packing to their rooms while also declaring quite vociferously that pretty soon one of them would be moved out of his room. It was, of course, nothing new. She always did that whenever she felt she had to take a decision on something that showed the world who she was. And she showed the world who she was and what her decisions were, by shuffling a random boarder.

The 'Bo' gang was baffled. It just didn't make any sense to them why they kept getting pulled. The last time they had got pulled, they were on a bike, riding out of the hostel campus. A rather trivial matter. By their standards, of course.

It was an evening when BoNO's flimsy physical frame was riding a bike which carried a lanky BoNuT, who kept his feet folded at the sides, along with a reasonably hefty BoNTree. With so much, the bike managed to behave itself with grace. It was a different matter that any pair of eyes that saw them from a distance and more specifically when Minal Borthakur's eyes saw them from a distance, it gave the impression of a trio of boys titter-tattering and riding a bike swerving it along the road at all the wrong places. And when it rode straight, a pair of folded feet made itself visible giving the bike the appearance of a vulture's wings as it sat hunched. Not to mention that the bulk of the second pillion threatened the front wheel of the bike to go up in the air.

When the bike with such precursory tendencies was met by the shining steel grey Innova of Minal Borthakur, it was unable to resist all temptations and forgoing all precautionary measures like brakes and shouting, indeed went front wheel up with the distinct intention of landing on the car. Had it not been for Minal's driver's James Bond inspired driving, there would have been a high decibel collision that would have been heavy on the wallet. Minal ma'am's wallet, that is. The bike belonged to some loafer who had loaned it to the Bo's' over a bottle of friendship the previous night.

And yet, the three could not help wondering **why** it was always them.

As for R&B, he took this whole episode pretty personally. He would show them who he was. That was a promise that Rajib Deka made to himself as he walked back to his hostel room.

7 IMRANPUR

The general belief was that a moghul king from the midlands of the country had dispatched an army to the north east with intentions of a conquest. The army was led by an officer named Imran. Lack of substantial proof has caused the lack of a general belief regarding this army's success which led to the belief that it was met with resistance and defeat everywhere it went.

It was in the course of such a journey that they reached a land very scenic in its beauty and sweet in its being. A land whose maidens and lads lived merrily making music with their heartbeats and laughter. *And* it was a land abundant in fish and water! With so much freshness all around, it was irresistible for Imran and his men to pitch a resting camp. After all, even defeated fallen heroes need to rest if they intend to return home in one piece.

Here though, there has been substantial proof that they had different thoughts when it came to 'returning home'. Like, mingling with the locals, mildly at first and intensively later, that more often than not led to marrying amongst them which in turn led to the inevitable arrival of little children…

This resting camp gradually turned into a mini settlement that eventually grew into a village with old man Imran as its chief. So naturally, when he died, the village decided to call itself Imranpur. What it was called before he died, no one appears to have bothered with. But then, there were the non believers and they disregarded this whole theory.

'Look,' they would say as they pointed to a rivulet flowing at one end of the place and continue, 'Here flows the Um Ryana', acknowledging the presence of the river goddess's daughter Ryana amidst them. 'Um', meaning 'river' in one of the local languages.

It was Her Supreme Command to have people guarding her, for she was once stolen by a thief from her mother's lap when the mother suddenly fell asleep. This village was the result of that guard. So, the name of the village was 'Umryanpur' and not what the moghul history crazy freaks had put it as.

Idiots.

And then, there were those other people at the University. The ones who buried themselves behind rows of books and theorized and debated all the time. They said, never mind the name. What was important was that, the village was a 'buffer zone' between the local chieftains and 'outside forces'; the 'outside forces' being the Moghuls, the Burmese, the Nepalese, the Japanese, the Chinese, the British, the Bangladeshis, the Biharis, the Bengalis, the disgruntled youths who had taken up arms and refuge in Bhutan, the national government and most recently, the state government. The port located at the far end of the village that housed records of having ferried rebels, prisoners, fighters and others was a proof of this, they declared.

Of the name, they conveniently credited it to the bunch of 'Imli' trees growing at the port. So the name, if it had to be anything at all, they said, was 'Imlipur'.

'But where are those trees?', the villagers asked.

Oh, they got washed away by the Brahmaputra during the great earthquake of the mid 1900s. Didn't they remember?

To ensure that future memories didn't turn deceitful and to prevent further knowledge raking on the matter, the village council decided that the village was best called 'Imry'. One day, it hired a daily wage labourer who, for fifty rupees-an-hour, walked up to the banyan tree growing at the approach to the main crossroad, the Imry Chariali, and hammered a tin card that had 'Imry Chariali Baas Stop' inscribed on it. That settled the matter. The most that they would tolerate was an 'Umry'.

Anything else would invite the most unwelcome of actions.

8 THE RIDE TO IMPRANPUR

I set out for Imranpur on the following Saturday early in the evening when the weather made tolerable the humid and heat, not to mention the fatigue, that set in from traveling. 'I will drop you', offered my Aunt. 'Nah! I will go by myself.'

'You will get lost', she reasoned. I gave her my 'Oh, yea?' look that didn't make me appear any more pretty than having pushed up my eyes, wrinkled my nose and pulled down my lips. It was my way of getting things, well, in my way.

'Stop that!' Aunt commanded slapping me on my head. 'This is not your Benga-lu-ru', she said. I stopped but purely out of surprise that she thought Bengaluru was a place for gaining prominence. To me it had always appeared to be a city where everyone had the same aspirations and lived the same life. People even appeared to be the same!

'Don't expect me to come searching for you if you get lost.'

'Of course not; why would you?'

I caught Aunt looking at me with steely eyes at that one. It took me a minute to realize what I had just said. It was our usual banter that would still have been our usual banter, but just that now there was the letter that kept playing at the background in our everyday life. Ever since I had told her about it, I felt she had started to go a little uncertain on our conversations, at times. Or perhaps that was my thinking.

But at that moment, I knew that she did go downcast on those last words. 'You can pack my bags and drive them there.' I said hugging her. 'Of course! After all I am your courier service!', she replied lunging to pull my ears. But I had already dived and disappeared into the shower shouting out that she also pack a few boxes of her cookies and cakes.

So now that Aunt had already helped with the transport of my luggage the day before, I only had to transport myself to my quarters at the college campus. The public transport buses would suffice. It would give me a better insight and connect to the place which was going to be my home and work place for quite sometime from now.

I took a bus from Baritola where Aunt stayed to Jalukbari, the last suburb of the city, best known for housing the state's first engineering college, the Assam State Engineering College (ASEC). Here, the State Transport Corporation ended its services which meant that to go any further; I had to opt for the 'Mezic' and 'Trakkar' service.

Small and medium mini TATA Magic and Trekker vans in red, white and silver colour were lined along the road, close to the bus bay. This was the Magic and Trekker service that had become 'Mezic' and 'Trakkar' service. Much like it was 'Riks' for the folks, instead of 'Risk'. Conductors of these vans went about shouting the routes they would be plying on, as they gathered their passengers.

'Chariali, khali gaari!'

'Chariali khali garee!!'

I caught hold of one of them to enquire which one was for Imry Chariali. He pointed to the lot of Mezics parked a little distance away. I walked up to one asking, 'Khali garee?' quite clear that I would board only a near empty or just getting full 'Mezic'. 'Khali garee', the conductor confirmed.

I got into it. A man and a woman were already sitting inside. I took a seat opposite to them. We had to wait till all the seats were filled and after a much patience testing wait, our last passenger came, in the form of a short thin man of fragile frame who had wrapped a *gamusa*, the white bodied red patterned Assamese traditional cloth, around his head like a bandana and carried three large jute bags. He placed two of them below our seats- mine and his- while the third he put between the seats. Now set, we started off only to be waved to a halt by a group of boys. I wondered where they would fit in. Apparently, it was also a concern for the driver and conductor.

They refused to let them in.

The boys objected.

They protested.

The boys were amused at this and much to the chagrin of the driver and the conductor, the fellows swung themselves by the foot boards on the side and back of the trekker and yelling cheerfully at the passersby, asked the driver to get moving.

The conductor, himself swinging on one of the side doors, was venting his rage at the boys, reminding them that the last time they had attempted this, they had received blows from the traffic cops who rode past them decidedly with the intention of aiming their sticks at their behinds. To this the boys laughed and whistled before responding that should it happen this time, they would climb up to the roof of the vehicle. That left the conductor pretty much dumbfounded and muttering under his breath, while the boys began to sing and make merry along the ride

Inside, the driver decided to keep us entertained by playing music. Given the selections in his repertoire, I didn't feel entertained. Outdated racy bollywood numbers that were poorly written and composed never did.

The ride to Imry was of forty five minutes and as yet only fifteen minutes had passed. I was wondering how I would make it when I felt something pressing against my leg. I looked down to find that it was the large size jute bag of the *gamusa* banded man sitting next to me. I pushed it a little away with my leg only to find it pressing back again. Annoyed, I looked at the man hoping my annoyed glances would deliver the message. But he didn't take any notice.

However, after a few minutes, he popped his head out of the window and spit a mouthful of betel nut juice onto the road. Thereafter, turning to me, he grinned revealing his set of pan stained teeth.

'They are fresh from the market.' He said. 'What?' I asked shuddering at the thought whether the 'freshness' he was referring to was his teeth or the juice that he just spat out. 'Have a look' he continued, proceeding to part the opening of the jute bag.

Three duckling heads popped out and stared at me. 'Nice!' I said greatly relieved at the sight of the heads, of course. 'I have bought a cock also. He is sitting under your seat. It was very cheap in the market today.'

'Good for you!' I said, trying to convey that this was the most I would have of poultry related conversations and of my co passengers as well. I suffered a mild shock from trying to guess what the bird beneath my seat might have been thinking. For I had much to suffer in case it got any kind of funny idea and I was not very sure if its sense of humour matched mine.

By now we had left the city limits and were heading steadily towards Imry and the other villages that lay beyond it. The route was heavily dotted with numerous beels- rain water fed ponds- that had now increasingly become silt laden ponds, thanks to the flood waters from the river. Beyond, the Himalayan mountain range made itself visible in a bluish light that gave it an air of myth and enchantment, as the last rays of the sun danced on them. The air felt fresher and cooler. Being nauseated and tired by all the excitement in the van, it lulled me to sleep.

When I woke, I found myself alone in the Trekker. It seemed to have halted at some place. I saw a group of people a little distance away.

Worried that I might have slept past my destination, I got off the vehicle and went to enquire at the crowd that had assembled. As I got close to them, I recognized them to be my co passengers. For I could spot the duck-cock-*gamusa* man amongst them. Apparently there was some interesting development.

We were awaiting clearance from six young calves sitting in a line across the road, literally chewing the cud. Their bovine elders were trying to coax them to stand up and get going. No doubt, a noble intention. Just that it was a painstakingly slow process from their point of view and pretty time consuming from ours.

Despite these sincere efforts, there was no progress made. Seeing the elders fail in fulfilling their obligation, those cheerful boys who were free riding on our Trekker, got into action. They volunteered for physical intervention and lifting each of the calves up on their shoulders, transferred them to the green fields on the other side of the road.

All of us passengers naturally felt pretty grateful to them and I think it scored them a few brownie points with the conductor also, for he was no longer giving them any dirty looks. And when the boys got off at their stop, he announced quite volubly, in his gruff voice, that while this time he wouldn't charge them a paise, the next time they tried to swing onto his 'Trakkar', he would double charge them. To which the boys squealed a 'hobo de, will see!' and walked off singing tunelessly.

A few moments after that, the Trekker stopped in front of a banyan tree that had a tin card dangling on its stump. It read- Imry Chariali Baas Stop. This was the Imry crossroads junction, I was told. I had arrived in Imranpur finally!

Gladly paying the fare, I got out. If initially I had second thoughts on foregoing my aunt's offer, I was now glad of having done that.

This was indeed some trip, wow!

9 FIRST IMPRESSIONS

Imranpur or Imry as it is commonly called, is a village. At least, that is what it is as per the public opinion. For, when I told a friend of mine that I was heading to Imry to take up my new job, I was met with a 'Since-when-did-you-become-a-village-idiot' look. The villagers, of course, have a different opinion. They regard it to be a tiny city. I couldn't care less even if it were a village masquerading as a city. It wouldn't change my decision to go there. I wasn't going to devote time debating on its status. It didn't make any sense to do so.

Having arrived the day before and after sleeping well the first night at the faculty quarters, I decided to explore the place the following morning.

After a short tour, I concluded that the place is a village *aspiring* to be a city. Though, I have also felt momentarily that perhaps, it was actually a city reduced to the status of a village. On third thoughts, perhaps it was a village deliberately set up by market forces with the sole intention of creating a new playground to sell their wares using new strategies.

For I noticed, that there was one best shop for any purchase to be made. One best shop for cakes, one best shop for dresses, one best shop for groceries, one best bank to offer the best loans to buy cars from the one best dealer and even one best Magic Service for travel, which I got to check out since I arrived in Imry traveling on one of its carriers.

Everything fits so well. It is easier to create a village. City dwellers would crib and demand; villagers would accommodate and get along. For the former, more is forever less. For the latter, less is at times, an excess. Especially when it came to consumer products.

In fact, the very definition of fast moving consumer goods in itself was different for them. I realized this when I entered a shop to buy some biscuits. This shop literally sold everything under the sun and that included a few low end garments for both men and women. As I proceeded with making my purchase, I overheard an argument between a customer and the shop keeper.

The buyer side had bought a tee shirt that wore out within two wears and every subsequent exchanges made by the seller to satisfy the customer produced no different result. Each of them wore out. Frustrated, the customer arrived to declare that he would no longer be purchasing any more of these rotten fast moving consumer goods.

The shopkeeper was alarmed. Something stirred in him that made him desperately want to clear this misconception. He dutifully pointed out that not all things that are speedily exchanged or bought are fast moving consumer goods.

'Nonsense', muttered the customer. Anything and everything that moved between the buyer and seller is fast moving consumer goods. He argued. 'No', objected the shopkeeper. 'Some fall under Consumer Durables.' He also went on to clarify that, if after purchase of these items, they failed to register with the buyer, they did become Consumer Perishables. In the event of this happening, no shop or brand would take lifelong responsibility for it.

The customer was crestfallen. Nevertheless, he agreed to withdraw from the situation. But not before declaring that he was never going to purchase any more of these fast perishing consumer goods.

'Does that happen a lot?' I enquired, as I made my payment. The shopkeeper nodded. Well, well. Imry sure was going to offer lots to me.

10 THE BLESSED OF IMRANPUR

Anil, the Thikedar, was one of those 'Been there, Done that' characters that life throws at you every once in a while. While the masses at Imry seldom bother to analyze and rationalize the mechanics of success that comes to one of their own, in this case though, they had chosen to differ. There were broadly two schools of thoughts on this Thikedar character.

One portrayed him as the chosen son of the family and future of the village, on whom the local Goddess had chosen to bless in plentiful and whom, in turn, he had sought to patronize. The other, though, looked upon him as that ambitious young man who networked and schemed around to have things his way. It would not take much to figure out that the trigger for this chain of opinion was pure jealousy.

For you see, there were other 'faithful' of the Goddess who had even named their businesses after Her but they did not seem to have been able to invoke Her Blessed Hand. The most prominent of these failures being the rechristening of 'Joi Maa Magic Service' to 'Bhupen Magic Service'. Not that the fellow Bhupen regarded himself in the same esteem as the Holy Mother. But when days, weeks and months of using Her Name did not yield results, he had to take a call and this was the call he could think of to take. And going by the fact that his revenues did shoot up after this, he did seem to have a point as well.

But to keep the Thikedar's point always afloat, there was his mother. The aged old woman never lost a chance to extol the virtues of her son and cite them as the reasons for his success. If she never lost her chances, neither did the opposing faction lose theirs and from time to time would render out a warning to her. 'Watch out O *Burrie*! That old mouth is giving off more words than it can hold!' There were no signs of her heeding it.

To what extent the Thikedar himself was aware of these, one cannot say. For sometimes, his actions violated the 'Handpicked by Goddess to be Smiled Upon' image. Like the time when he offered ten '*sagoli puwalis*' in sacrifice to the Goddess when a 'deal' had come through. He had offered goat kids numbering ten in total.

'We can't even afford one and he gave ten *sagoli puwali*!' The villagers told one another. '*Burrie*, you must invite us to lunch', they told his mother who laughed her gruff laughter loudly and offered to send them some of the '*bhog*', offering from the temple. At other times he simply did not live up to the notions of a third class business agent. So, the public opinion for Anil Thikedar always remained balanced. He skewed it, whenever it suited him.

Right then, he was sitting in the cashier's seat at the Dunlop Hill Restaurant, chewing paan. He was sitting with a tray of paper napkins and a bowl full of flavoured saunf put at either end of the counter. Dunlop was his first foray into the world of food business. In its previous avatar, it was a roadside shop that allowed hungry passing by travellers to savor rice and fish curry sitting on wooden stools and tables.

In its current avatar, it was still on the same roadside but took advantage of the fact that the land was considerably raised in that area. So, it justified its existence on a 'Hill', by making it a part of its name. The Thikedar had bought it out and transformed it into a most sought after food hub amongst the college going crowd. It was a different matter that the crowd came from only one college and that was because there was only one college between Dunlop and the main, actual city.

The new offerings were plenty. Though, the menu had enough potential to drive away prospective customers by offering them 'Motor Penir' and 'Sicken Curry'. Otherwise, for the brave, bold and experimental foodie, Dunlop offered a colourful interior complete with Neelkamal furnishings, colour TV, uninterrupted FM radio music and the nearly always available internet.

It was in this current location that Anil Thikedar sat chewing paan. His eyes were fixed at something insignificant at a distance and a disturbing conversation kept playing over and again inside his head.

Early that morning, Rubul, his star performer had come to him to inform that he wouldn't work for him anymore. On being asked 'Why', he replied that it was 'On health grounds'. There, the actual conversation had ended. But not within the grey interiors of the Thikedar's head.

He knew Rubul was lying.

He knew that the 'health ground' reason was an excuse.

He knew that he had offered the best of what he could.

Yet, he could not do anything about it.

Apart from paying him his fee, he paid for Rubul's accommodation, travel, food and in addition, even managed to make him the brand ambassador for Dulce & Gabber, a new fashion line that was fast becoming a rage in Imry. How much more could you do for a part time actor of the traveling village theatre, wondered the Thikedar.

He knew it wouldn't make sense to even Rubul himself, if he was going to join his rival who could never beat his pay. So he really didn't get it when Rubul told him he was quitting.

Also, he was worried. He had just got into the entertainment business. By Goddess, he had begun on a high. But now with the crowd puller gone, he had to ensure that his average earnings per show was enough to meet the expenses, even if it did not fetch profits. And for that, he needed a replacement. Where could he find one?

He spit the juice from the existing paan and started on a new one. Every fresh thought, needs a fresh paan. That's the motto with the Thikedar.

Sarat, the actual cashier at Dunlop had once mentioned a name to him. Actually, it was Sarat's friend working as a security guard at the Institute, who knew this fellow. He couldn't recollect it now. He would have to wait for him to come. The man was already late by three hours. The Thikedar looked at the wall clock put over the *gamusa* that was hung above the chair. He was hoping that Sarat was just being late. That he wasn't the next quitter in his list.

11 A NEW BEGINNING

Antony lay on his bed with his hands folded under his head. From this vantage point, he had approximately a 270 degree view of the college campus. But he chose to focus on the roof of the Administrative Block. Beside him lay his now totally uncool phone on which he had logged on to Facebook where his updated status read, 'Tony Baruah- feeling Meh'.

It was altogether a different matter that he did not know what feeling 'Meh' was all about. All that he knew was that he wasn't feeling happy about the way things were going and certainly not optimistic about how things looked posed to be. And for him, that was enough to feel 'Meh'.

Outside, the rain clouds that had gathered since the afternoon finally broke and pour into a drizzle while undisciplined breeze moving at non periodic intervals dispersed the chill that had gathered as a consequence of the downpour. He blinked hard at the roof. But no, it wasn't the roof that he was interested in. It was the train of thoughts that was associated with it that he was mentally engaged in. He was recollecting the build up to the day that he had aborted the jump- off from that building.

Had he been chicken hearted one more time because he had backed out? He still wasn't able to make up his mind on that. Another proof that he was living a useless life. When did he notice it for the first time?

At his first stage performance. With the school choir. Where he played his tabla standing behind all the singers completely blocked from the audience's view. The tablist schoolboy's early musical career was entirely spent on being an accompanist to prayer songs sung during the morning assembly. It didn't get anymore starrier than that.

He thought that perhaps life would change for the better when he entered college. At least that was what he had been assured of. But it was not to be.

All that the college crowd cared for was stuff that came tagged with the 'Devil-may-care' attitude mixed with a dash of glamour. Clearly, the tabla didn't fit in with this image. It lost effortlessly to the mighty drums, followed by the guitar. The only hopes of salvaging some reputation lay in the hope that there would be a fusion of Eastern and Western music. But alas, that was not to be, either.

To make matters worse, Tony's tabla acquired the reputation of being the only percussion instrument in the whole of the village. A record previously held by the dumroo of the monkey dance master. But ever since the monkey ran away – might have been captured by the government as well- the position lay vacant. The villagers were missing the sound of this marvelous device that could inspire an ape to dance and were happy to have found an alternative to it in Tony's tabla. Tony, however, didn't appreciate this.

Music was Tony's heart and soul; the very ingredient of his living. But feeling deprived of its joy, he failed to see any meaning in his existence.

Getting added to this was his unsatisfactory academic performance at the Institute of Technical Education. It was another line in life which he had never wished to pursue but was forced to. To top it all, there was the case of Gitusmita who had dumped him rather unceremoniously ever since she had heard the guitarist sing and perform at the Inter Departmental gathering. Though officially named Fardin, he had christened himself as 'The King' and styled himself along his punch line, 'Fardin, The F- Factor'.

That afternoon, as he danced all over the stage dressed in a fish net shirt and his trademark cut-paste jeans wear crooning into the microphone, he suddenly stopped. Then, jumping off the ramp, he landed in the midst of the audience and walking up to Gitusmita, went down on one knee and said, 'Here's your King, baby! Don't make me crazy but be my Queen, Lady!', looking straight into her eyes. Following which he ran up the stage with the intention of serenading 'Come, Let Us Not Go Home Tonight'.

However, after he sang the first two lines of this highly suggestive song, he spotted Minal Borthakur fidgeting at her seat which immediately gave rise to suspicions in The King's mind that perhaps she had objections to the song and borne out of this, she might consider catching hold of the Dean and come up to the stage to admonish him. Not wanting to spoil the sentiments of the occasion, he hastily changed into the hazard free, Down The Country Road, suffering badly at the hands of the audience who booed relentlessly at being cheated; with someone even going to the extent of howling that he might as well have sung 'Mary Had a Little Lamb' while another somebody created a lot of sarcastic laughter by passing the suggestion that at this rate, The King would sing 'Ba Ba Black Sheep' at his wedding.

But that did not stop another section of the audience from letting their emotions run high. *The girls.*

Barring the exceptions, of course. They fluttered their eyes and cooed around Gitusmita telling her what a lucky girl she was! Though, if anyone would have looked straight into *their* eyes, they would have seen jealousy streaming ferociously.

Of the boys, the ones who had attained wisdom on these matters by giving away their hearts to just about every damsel that they saw howled a smattering of encouragement for The King. Even though they knew that, this too shall pass. In all likelihood, it had to do with their fraternal tendencies that gave them this sense of responsibility.

The remaining were full of contempt. For the very simple reason that a standard had *now* been set. And nothing short of that was going to impress *their* girls. They could already feel the pressure coming on. Damn, 'The King'!

Only BoNuT, BoNTree and BoNO were detached of the show. They were old hands at this- the singing, that is. Though from time to time one or the other Bo did get fanciful ideas of a beauty. Also, they were the seniors of the college. So they knew that this wasn't going to get anywhere beyond the boundaries of *this* college. For one thing, they were not impressed by his lyrics writing skill. What was this nonsense about 'not going home at night'?

'I Have a Sinner's Soul', was more of their forte. Also, for the life of them they could not understand why The King chose to sing his songs always a pitch low, which no doubt gave the renditions an unmusical twist. That, despite this handicap, he had managed to score points with a girl was of no consequence to them. They exchanged meaningful glances and decided to give His Unmelodious Highness a pass. Besides, despite being seniors, they still had that Chemistry Part 2 exam from a lower semester, to clear the next morning.

All of which meant that the proceedings of the evening had left only one person evidently heartbroken. Tony Baruah. In a flash of a second, he saw all the gifts, cards, cakes and chocolates that he had given Gitusmita from his savings of five rupee changes collected from the Trekker travels for his table lessons go out of the window.

Everyone. Everyone, in the college had a 'ga-ga' factor to them. Except Tony. He was the 'pooh-pooh' factor. During the Fresher's Party, in addition to The Most Desirable Guy award, won by The King, had there been a Most Pooh-Pooh-able Guy category, then Tony would have won it hands down flat.

They 'pooh-poohed' him every weekend when he travelled to Guwahati for his tabla classes. And they 'pooh-poohed' him on the week days when he sat down to practice. One chap even took the efforts of mimicking him by banging on the door simultaneously. But since he had no sense of rhythm, he kept getting out of sync only to create successfully a din that brought out the warden who launched into one of his long discipline laden sermons. All of this made Tony feel ashamed. And they 'pooh-poohed' him again on the day of Saraswati Puja when he dressed up in a dhoti and went to pay his respects to his guru and then sit down in front of the Goddess's idol to play.

Their jeering rang so deeply in his ears late into the night that then and there Tony took his decision- if things weren't getting starrier for him, then it was time that he got starrier instead. He decided he would campaign for himself about his own goodness and win his friends. A thought that led him to creating the 'Tak Dhina Dhin with Tony' page on Facebook that would tell the story, the ups and downs of an aspiring boy table player. But his stardom was short spanned by a mere three Page likes and no comments.

He should have learnt from the movies. Had he seen any of the young heroes making it big in reel life thanks to a tabla? No. He should have swapped long time back. Now that he hadn't, he was paying various amounts of prices at several installments.

Tony knew the reason.

It was too late but he realized that this was his tabla's doing as well. His choice of instrument itself was grossly wrong. He sought comfort in the thought that it could have been far worse than this. What if his folks had made him learn the harmonium instead? He shuddered to think if there would have been any prospects at all, in that case.

The prospects weren't great at the moment either. Right then, he wished he could turn into a free bird, flap his wings and fly away from that hostel room. Or may be a kite. A kite was better. Not only could he just fly away, he could also 'cut' other kites along the way. But, the improbability of both added another drop of sadness in his life.

He had tried breaking free from this rut, once. On that evening after the Inter Departmental gathering. After it had got over, he went home rather than going back to the hostel where he was sure he could not get himself to stand the after talk of the evening's King moment.

He lay quietly on his bed with a hand over his grieving heart and ear phones plugged onto his ears. The well mannered boy that he was brought up to be, he sought to take solace in music rather than at the street side shady shop at Imranpur that sold questionable quality of drinks till early morning or smoke the night away at the snookiest corner of the hostel with equally snooky fellows for company who would share their share their quota of broken hearts saga.

Eventually, he fell asleep oblivious that a few feet from the bed where he lay, stood his father looking at him with such fondness that only a father whose hard work, dedication and discipline to mastering music could have. And Tony would have continued receiving such fond looks from his father as he kept sleeping, had it not been for a hard hitting slap on his face that woke him up.

It was his Father. Something seemed to have suddenly snapped the fondness he was feeling for his son. The man was looking at his son with fiery eyes. Waging a finger, he raged in anger. 'That is not what I gave you that phone for. That is not what I put my money in for!'

It took Tony sometime to figure out what his father was fussing at. When his senses cleared, he realized that his father was referring to the iPhone. It was a gift that an image conscious father had given to his son so that he didn't suffer from any jibes of being over traditional. Much the same reason that he had given an extra, zing sounding name as well- Antony.

As a leading musician of his day, he had accompanied accomplished dancers and singers from the state on their national and international tours. So he had learnt quickly that learning the ancient classics had to be integrated with modernity. That meant giving his son a phone on which he could listen to recorded classical music, which was extremely modern by his thinking because in his time, phones were used only for talking to one another. Shouting, rather.

What he did not expect the phone to do was feed FM radio music to his son, on whom he had hopes of grooming a fine artist to carry on his name. What he actually found it doing was even more blasphemous. It was playing a disco song that claimed that the water today is blue, blue, blue.

Now, Mr. Kamala Kanta Baruah may have been a musician in heyday. But he also had got himself a degree in the basic sciences and even without that he had the common sense about the colour of water. So he was not going to have his son's musical abilities and intellect be spoilt by a pedestrian singer who seemed to have bunked his elementary chemistry lessons at school and therefore sang about the water being blue in colour.

But Tony was in no mood to being trashed about, questioned or willing to debate or implore forgiveness. That evening- dear readers-he was a young chap who had been betrayed by his maiden. He was broke and he was angry. He had to take it out. And he took it out by going against his father.

Rounds of angry exchanges, arguments, bickering and debating consequently brought a point where the father challenged his son's intelligence by asking for his academic progress and it proved him to be right. *Tony had scored a red mark in one subject.*

The irony was that it was in chemistry, causing the father to exclaim that no wonder these days the water was blue. Thoroughly dejected and vanquished, Tony threw away the phone and at the first sight of morning light, left for the hostel.

'You can put that blame on me', he muttered to himself as he looked at the poster of his idol, an African rapper whose musical existence was a well kept secret in the Baruah household. He knew that this is exactly the piece of advice that his idol would have given him, had he asked him in person. But the fixed gaze from that static image that was taped to the wall under the tube light also met with the expectations and hence sufficed.

The Idol's philosophy was that ideally whoever is responsible, should own up, else volunteer to do so. Just like The Idol had himself done once. He was accused of robbery and some ungentlemanly behaviour towards the ladies (Deeds K.K Baruah would most certainly not approve of) for which obviously his sponsors had no obligation to take ownership of (Deeds K.K Baruah would most certainly approve of), but which The Idol felt otherwise. Anyway, he had apologized and matters had cooled. His fan following was back. (Matters on which K.K Baruah would have reserved his humble opinion) And one of them by the name of Tony was absolutely adoring him at the moment. (A matter K.K Baruah was in the dark about).

Convinced that he had done 'the needful', Tony felt consoled. Picking up his cell phone, he logged onto Facebook, to update his profile and state what was on his mind.

Tony Baruah went from 'In a complicated relationship' to 'Single'.

Tony Baruah has finally figured how to move on.

On the feelings front though, he continued to feel 'Meh'.

Here, he was interrupted by the knocking at his door. That reminded him, he was to get a new roommate that evening. Tony went to open the door hoping that whoever the new 'he' was, 'he' would be half as decent as himself. He had enough of the Hostel In Charge's shifting roommates business.

On the other side of the door, a confident Rajib Deka waited patiently to be let in with his belongings.

12 AT THE COLLEGE

The Dr B.N Saikia lab on the third floor of the West Wing, Administrative Block, wore a deserted look. Or rather, it appeared as if it had been deserted. At least that is how I found it when I arrived there the following morning. I had been told to report to Sudhir at the Department of Electronics & Communication Engineering which was the Dr B. N Saikia lab, and there I was.

From the state of the room, it certainly did appear that it had been occupied. I could see books on desks, the CROs- both the bulky and sleek kinds- on the lab table and shelves where rows of components stood bottled and labeled. On one particular table, the particularly voluminous 'Microelectronics Devices by Sedra & Smith' lay open and the chair pulled afar, conveying as if whoever had been sitting on it and reading had been suddenly summoned off. And given that the large glass windows had been pulled aside, granting full access to an uninterrupted view of lush green fields ahead, a person of spirited disposition was likely to conclude that the occupants of the room had made along that route in a hurry. The still running fans would have supported the theory.

A little Alice-in-wonderland-esque.

But the maximum that I could do was conclude that it was a scene fit enough to be featured in an Agatha Christie mystery which meant that if I looked down from that open window, *I might find a body.* In my mind, I saw the title and the cover page of this new book- The

Body in the Lab. Excited by my own thoughts, I walked up to the window and peered out of it. A solitary cow stood below chewing the cud.

I sighed guessing that I had to search for some entertainment elsewhere. Better to look around the lab for now.

My eyes went over the shelves of components and equipments where resistors, capacitors, diodes all jostled for space. A few were scattered on a nearby lab table that also had a soldering iron and a few circuit boards scattered around. It hinted at the strong probability that perhaps there was the odd incident of a boy and/ or girl student who had scalded fingers with that soldering rod and screamed down the place making it appear as if the lab was some kind of a torture room. Young blood with attention seeking capabilities was quite capable of doing this, and more.

I picked up a resistor. I never really liked the capacitors for their flimsy legs or the diodes for the confusion they posed with their positive and negative ends. And anyway, a resistor was colourful and amusing.

However, I was not the only one to find resistors this attractive. Ages before me, someone had been so fascinated by the colour rings around them that he/ she had dedicated a very poignant phrase about it that went as, B B Roy has a Very Beautiful wife Wearing Gold and Silver Necklace. This electronic intellect enhancing, mark scoring, lab experiment output guaranteeing nugget of wisdom regarding the value of resistance coded in the coloured rings was passed on from professor to student, generation after generation ever since **anyone** could remember. I had received it from mine as a student and now here I was to dispense it to the current crop of students pursuing all streams of engineering.

But, seeing that quite a number of B B Roys and their Very Beautiful wives along with their Gold and Silver Necklaces had been soldered into the circuit boards, I wondered if I had been spared of that obligation. Finding little else to keep myself interested in, I stepped out of the lab onto the corridor.

I could not find anyone immediately. Though, a minute or so later, I did see Minal Borthakur walking up. I recognized her from my meeting with her the previous evening when she had come on a courtesy visit intended to show me around the premises and most importantly the staff quarters. I waved her a Hello and wished her a Good Morning. She returned the salutations duly and apologized for not being able to stay back for a chat as she was on her way to get the Dean since an urgent matter of discipline had come up. I let her carry on and returned to the lab.

Grabbing a stool, I sat near the window. Until someone or something turned up, all that I could do was admire the view on offer- a cow with the fields beyond it, beyond which was a half filled river with a fractured wooden bridge that let the daily traffic ply about and the mountains in the distance. It would now be a matter of minutes before I would drift into a dreamy state where I would see myself climbing those mountains and when I reached the summit, be greeted by Daddy and *another man*. 'Your father, Gigglepot', he would say.

However, I was deprived of attaining this mental state when, merely a few seconds later, I heard a joyful exclamation next to me. 'Ah!' it went.

'You must be Ashima, the new assistant professor we have been waiting for.' I turned around to find a young man standing with keenness to ask questions and get answers. There was a certain freshness in his voice that went well with the sincerity that his face covered by a mop of curled hair radiated and completing the joy that emanated, were his sunken eyes that vanished on smiling.

'I am.' I confirmed. 'I am Sudhir.' He introduced himself and we shook hands. While it was indeed flattering to know that my presence was longed for, I couldn't help enquiring into the reason. For one thing, I had no prior reputation as a teacher, let alone a much sought one. Sudhir told me that it was because they were short of staff. More specifically since he himself was on the short end, having to shunt between two colleges- one where he was teaching and one he was himself a student in post doctoral studies.

'Hope you have not been waiting for long,' he said after he had clarified my doubts. 'Actually there was some -' he hesitated here, trying to find a right word to continue. 'You could say, strange development with the students', he finished, deciding that this was the best possible way to summarize it.

'Oh, what was it?' I was curious, further telling him of my short conversation with the Hostel In-Charge who gave me the impression of some sort of undisciplined behavior having taken place. 'You could put it that way too.' Sudhir agreed before going on to narrate what actually had happened. A brand new bike had been discovered at the back of the Boys' Hostel.

'And that's not allowed?' I asked.

Sudhir told me that had permission been taken, it could have been allowed if the reasons were valid. But it would have to be parked in the garage, not behind the hostel. And that is what aroused suspicion. Especially because even the security could not answer when it came in and what it was doing there. Discreet enquiries revealed that 'A Boy' occupying a ground floor room at the Boy's Hostel had purchased it himself. This gave rise to more suspicions as 'A Boy' was not known to be apt in monetary dealings. So obviously everyone from the Head of the Institute to the Hostel Management to the teachers and the peons and the security, however incompetent the latter, were interested to know how 'A Boy' had managed it.

In depth enquires which included the parents of 'A Boy' went on to establish some shocking revelation, which so deeply affected the parents that the mother fainted and the father went speechless. It had turned out that 'A Boy' had stolen the money that his father had recently withdrawn from bank for some matter and then gone ahead and made his purchase of the two wheeler. It also emerged from the gossip quarters that the remaining money was spent entertaining a girl friend.

'We asked the father what is to be done', said Sudhir. I must admit I was also curious to know this. 'What did he say?' I asked. 'He asked us to report it to the police because he declared then and there that such a boy could not be his son and so he was disowning him.'

'And then?'

'Well, the Head felt that would be bad publicity. Besides, he felt that would be like washing the family's dirty linen in public.' However exciting the prospect of going public on the matter was, I too could not agreed more on the decision that the Head took. And given the dirtiness of the linen, I was quite sure that a lot of the public would be interested in joining hands for its washing.

'Anyway, it was the security's fault. What was he doing there when this bike was being smuggled?'

I agreed to that one too. Apparently the Head was more concerned with that, since Hostel Security was also part of Hostel Management. But the latter thought otherwise. And together they all agreed that it was the family values at fault. So it was to sort out who was to be blamed for what and why and an action plan on 'What Next' that there was a quick conference with the Head, the senior teachers, hostel management and of course, the Dean.

'But all that is sorted now.' Sudhir assured me. I was very glad of that. I didn't want my teaching stint to begin with this kind of impression of my would-be students. I already found this episode too melodramatic for comfort. A sorted lot would be so much easier to deal with.

13 THE START OF SOMETHING NEW

For my benefit, Sudhir explained to me that I had joined at the end of the ongoing semester. Which meant that for now all that I would be doing is invigilating the exams. Currently, the semester end exams were being held. That would be followed by a month or little more of break time during which I could prepare myself for the next semester. 'And in that time you can meet the remaining faculty from our department as well. Most generally don't come during these invigilation days', said Sudhir. This meant that the business of invigilating mainly fell on only a handful of those who were willing to undergo this kind of baptism by fire.

To me this seemed most certainly as an agreeable situation too. After all, there was much that I myself had to revise, that went beyond the Bengali surnamed mister whose jewellery loving wife never seemed to have enough of getting decked up in gold and silver jewellery.

What did not suit me was invigilating a set of students appearing for their mathematics exam regarding me as a walking encyclopedia on the subject and therefore asking me all of their doubts. Worse, they framed their doubts in such a fashion that it could only elicit the direct answer to the question asked. This much, I figured out. I tried getting away by asking them to wait for their maths teacher to come by. But they were too wily to fall for that. And although on the face of it, they all seemed to have got back to solving the paper, I had a feeling that something disagreeable was going on, to which I could not put my finger on.

I was especially guarded about one boy who appeared to get dreamy when he looked into the question paper and then very poetic when looking into his own answer sheet. To supplement these emotions, he was also waving his arms about randomly and babbling to himself. I had never known maths to have such ecstatic influence on its students.

'That sounds like Tanmoy', concluded Debhargya, the physics teacher who I met over the tea break, mid way during the examination. He had accepted it as his fate that he was not teaching a class of potential Noble Laureates in that area of science. His statement was supported by Hiramoni, the teacher in chemistry who provided her own two bits saying, 'That boy is unsound.'

This teacher had it in her, to regard the entire department of physics as her professional rival, so much that for every student they flunked in an exam, she flunked twice the number merely to advertise that hers was a tougher subject and that she was an even more academically particular teacher. Besides, she had a 'foreign' degree which necessitated her need to let her differentiation show. So naturally, she went one up on her remarks on Tanmoy by going on to narrate an episode that involved this boy. It was an occasion where he had jumped the college fences at night and gone into a neighbour's house and beat him up after waking him up from sleep.

'I hate having to talk about students like him!' Exclaimed Madhobi, the maths teacher who let it be known that she had her tastes in who she chose to talk about and discuss. To prove it, she would do a round of the examination halls an hour later than required and then, she would only go to those students who fit in with her choices. 'It is about how they *are,* you know.' She explained.

Her discriminatory tendencies had earned her quite a reputation among the students and the faculty as well. With the faculty, it was more about 'how they *are dressed,* you know'. This was strictly observed with the lady members since there was much to observe and scrutinize as against none with the gentlemen.

As for the students, she had compartmentalized her mind and filled it with those who '*are good*' or '*is good*' and those who '*are not*' or '*is not*'. According to this classification, the '*is/are good*' were talented as well as…well, good, what else. Like that boy, Fardin whom she regarded as being the epitome of being 'is good' because he was talented, having composed his own song titled, 'A Hundred on Love's ABCD' and winning a prize for it too.

'Well, well, that seems to be the only subject he can score a hundred on', jutted Hiramoni ma'am. For apparently, he could not even identify, nay, spot the difference between a beaker and a test tube, let alone identify the chemicals and salts, during the lab exam. 'I had no option but to declare him failed.' She confessed holding up her hands to show her helplessness in the matter. That foreign degree had certainly played a role in sharpening her teaching ethics, even if it didn't win her any brownie points with the maths teacher. And physics had never mattered, anyway. For the rest of the break, we munched our samosas and sipped the gingered black tea in silence and then returned to our respective halls to resume our duties.

Once back, I hovered around Tanmoy's seat to try and find out if he was up to any funny business. He wasn't. He merely continued to flit in and out of his dual mental states. I managed to get a look at the covering sheet of his answer paper on the pretext of 'checking for the seal' and found that indeed, he *was* Tanmoy. Tanmoy Kumar. I decided that if Master Ecstasy Kumar was going to attempt anything unwarranted, I would have to train my wits on him.

Later, when I returned to the Dr. B. N Saikia lab after handing over the answer sheets, the tea-lady came along and whispered to me that the present batch of students were hopeless. 'Ye no miss?', she continued 'All they are doing is enzoi-ying. Bois wid da garls and garls with the bois.'

'It is their age to, baidou.' I said trying to provide some defence which I felt was not altogether wrong. She shook her head. 'Their mummis and daddis are paying for the studdis. But they are enzoi-yings!' She cried in disgust, shaking her head even more. I sent her off.

At that moment, even I wanted to shake my head and tell myself that I was not 'enzoi-ying' this. May be because my 'mummis and daddis' were not paying for this. But I *was* being paid after all. And because of that, perhaps I should shut up for the moment. I sat on my stool, sipping my tea and looking out of the window.

Ah, those mountains!

Perhaps, they wanted me to know the secret they kept behind what appeared as magic emeralds shrouded by clouds. What secret did they keep guard of? If I went through them, would they lead me unto another world?

I decided to ask around and find out if there were any trekkers or climbers or the like. It would be most welcoming to get on an occasional trek among them. And may be, one day, when I am exploring a leafy trail, I would suddenly come across a clearing where I would find a solitary grave…

Ah, what fanciful thought invigilating exams in a remote college can bring!

14 NEXT DOOR NEIGHBOURS

'You won't believe how lazy they are!' Exclaimed Minal Borthakur as she stood in the kitchen of my quarter, waving a branded handkerchief as she spoke while she examined the sink. I would. Much as I now believed what I had overheard the students say to each other about her, as I passed by them at the corridor. They were discussing a wobbling roof at the hostel that remained unfixed for more than a week causing them to make unsuccessful attempts to sleep, being disturbed by the disgruntling sounds it made. This lack of a week's sleep was now making them very grumpy and most crib-y, to the point that they claimed that Minal ma'am was only after making money —so she could do her shopping in Singapore-rather than provide the services for which she took that money.

Now, leaning on the wall of the kitchen with my arms crossed, I was more than willing to agree with those students. From the day that I had taken a look at the quarter with Aunt Sarah, I had been telling Minal ma'am that the kitchen sink leaks and I wanted it fixed before I moved in.

May be she did, maybe she didn't. But it didn't change the fact that by the evening of my first day's stay in the house, the sink was seeping out water, making the entire floor wet. So now I stood there holding Minal ma'am responsible for this, while she held the plumber guilty of being a cheat at work.

'Ma'am', I said as my disappointment changed to anger and morphed into stubbornness. 'I want this fixed in the next one hour'. The words came out almost as an ultimatum. Minal Borthakur regarded this in silence.

When we had first met, she had told me that it was her own experience of having worked in the corporate world that had given her this confidence on running her own business now, citing that 'Delivering Work' and 'Swiping Cards' were the top two things that she had learnt from this experience. However, from this kitchen episode, her ability to do the first had now become questionable and to be known only for the second, seemed a little embarrassing even to her own self. At least that is what I figured from the silence that followed after I had issued the deadline. But I was not going to be apologetic about it. Telling her to lock the door once she had got the work done, I went out.

A walk would be nice, I thought. There wasn't anything else to do. On the second floor of the building where my quarter was, there was just one other flat and that was as yet unoccupied. So, no chance of any socializing there. Besides, it was the country side and anyway I had not explored much after that little shopping expedition that I had undertaken upon arrival. A little walk never harmed anyone.

Right outside the staff campus, stood a set of houses that was part of the village land not taken over by the college. As I walked past them, I found a woman standing on the verandah of her house looking at me. She smiled.

'You must be new!' she shouted in Assamese across the compound wall that separated the house from the road. 'Hoi!' I confirmed.

'You are studying?'

'No.'

'You are doing service in that college, is it?'

'Yes.'

'One of my relatives is also with the college.'

'Oh!'

'My husband's sister's brother's son's friend.'

'Ok!'

'He drives the college bus.'

'Oh!'

'Why don't you come in and have tea?'

This invitation to tea was a sign that a bond had been formed. I had now been accepted into her inner circle of family, by virtue of being associated with something which one of their own was also a part of. In the distant future, I was also likely to face the risk of being declared as an obscure but relevant relation, figuring somewhere along their family tree.

'Actually I am going...' I didn't know where. '...for some purchase.' I quickly made it up. 'Then have tea on your way back.' A very persistent woman, I noted. I smiled, said 'Thank You,' and then added a 'Khuri'. The Assamese woman in her neighbourhood is always addressed as a 'Khuri'.

'Khuri', the paternal aunt if you knew her through her husband, who would then be, 'Your Khura'; 'Mahi', the maternal aunt, if you knew her first, in which case the husband would be 'Your Moha'; or you simply addressed her as 'Baidou', the elder sister if she was unmarried or if you didn't know her marital status or if you happened to randomly run into one, of which there was a high probability always since they were seen anywhere from the market, to the bus stop to any neighbourhood you were in.

'You are most kind!' I declared and continued walking, all the while feeling the woman's gaze follow me. Something about the woman struck me as odd. I didn't know what.

However, at four in the evening, walking on a road with paddy fields on both sides and a sun shining warmly, I was feeling my cheery self again, that put away the woman from my mind.

I had only gone a short distance, just beyond the banyan tree which housed a Shiva temple and stepped on the partly broken wooden bridge from where the College could be seen, when I found a group of little children standing knee deep in the river below fishing with their bare hands.

'Go fishing, Gigglepot?' daddy Brendon's voice suddenly rang in my ears. Of course.

That is what he would have done, had he been where I was standing. He used to bundle up Eddie, Amy and me and take us to the huge pond at the end of our bungalow at the tea estate on Sunday afternoons and wading into the water in his shorts, show us how to fish. Occasionally, a few of the workers' children also joined us. Then, he would give each of them a fish to carry home. He was always doing something like that to delight kids. No wonder then that he was quite popular as the 'Boga Saheb' Uncle –the White Sahib Uncle- amongst them.

I searched the pockets of my chinos to see if I had anything to give those fishing children. A couple of cough lozenges and lollipops were all that I could find. I put them together and waved at the children. They waved back. In my pony tail, floral top, chinos and sneakers, I must have appeared quite touristy in the milieu of dhoti-shirts and *mekhela-chadors*.

Deciding that I wanted to buy the fish that they had caught, the children scrambled ashore, up to the bridge and chattered excitedly in the local Imry dialect of Assamese. I tried my best in my broken city Assamese to tell them what my intentions were but they were lost on them and at the end of ten minutes, I found myself in the possession of seven fishes in return for the cough lozenges and lollipops.

'Hell, what do I do?' I said aloud.

'Cook and eat it, Ma-joni', came a voice from behind. I turned around to find the priest of the temple. His very appearance gave me an instant idea. Why not offer him a part of it? He hesitated. But a great believer in my own ideas, I persevered. 'Please consider it as my offering to the temple.' I said putting out two of the fishes. That worked. An offering to the temple always worked with the Assamese priest of the tantric clan.

With a burden now, I had no option but to walk back to my quarters. Just as I reached the gates, I realized that I didn't know how to clean up a fish. I considered going back and trying to find someone to do that for me, when it struck me that I had a new found neighbor who could help me out with it.

'Khuri!' I called out, standing at the gate of her house.

'Who is it?' She called back.

'Ashima, we met sometime back today.'

'Oh yes, I knew it! Just I didn't ask your name only!'

'I got fish.'

'How nice!'

I knew that I was being abrupt and a little selfish at the cost of sending out a wrong signal of wanting to further a friendship I was not particularly looking for. Quite tactless on such matters, I directly came to the point, asking her help while asking her to accept two of the fishes.

'So now you can have tea, no?'

There was no refusing now, given that drinking tea was the second best thing an Assamese could do after fishing or having anything to do with fish.

'Your sink is now fixed', she said as she laid out a tray of homemade coconut laddoos, biscuits and tea. Seeing the startled look on my face she continued, 'Roopom, that plumber who worked on it told me. He is a nephew from my brother's in-laws' side.'

'Oh! Nice to know that.' I said, adding a little later, 'You have a really large family, Khuri!'

She sighed. 'Oh yes! They are all there, living in their own houses all along this road. Mother's side, father's side, husband's side. You should have seen the crowd that had come for my *juroon*. My family did not know where to seat them only! And when they were handing me the presents, I just lost track of who is who!' She said, referring to her engagement. 'And yet look at me now! Only I know how lonely I am.'

'Your khura, is either working in his office or watching TV and my only son is either away in college or chatting with his friends. Men people can be such a bore!' I sipped my tea and took bites of the laddoos as she discoursed through.

'Are you married?' she asked unexpectedly. 'No, Khuri'. 'Oh!', her face fell before brightening up again as she added, 'Don't forget me to invite for your *juroon*!'

I was a little startled by her addiction for attending engagements. Before she decided to self invite herself for more events that were due for my future self or dig out more personal information, I quickly finished my tea and took her leave. 'Thank you very much Khuri! I must be going now. I have taken much of your time.'

'Oh, don't say that', she replied, taking my hands into hers. 'You must come again.' I smiled and withdrew my hands which she now held in a tight clasp. As I picked up the cleaned fish and stepped out into the road, Khuri called out. 'You have a new neighbour.'

Huh?

At this rate, I had a feeling this woman was going to beat Google and Bing put together, at being the fastest information provider.

15 SUNDAY

There is one particular time of the day when one man in Imranpur not only feels but knows, rather he is convinced, that he alone is the center of the universe. This hour comes without fail every day, at the same time, every month all round the year and through all seasons. His conviction is firm. And why not?

After all, at that hour, only he is awake and has the privilege of enabling the rest of the village to not just wake up but rise up to meet the challenges and opportunities of the day. At that hour, he paddles his bicycle, past rickshaw-wallahs dozing on their rickshaws in anticipation of being woken up by the first passengers for the day, wandering men snoring on newspapers spread out on the side steps of shops and street dogs curled up under old battered cars put out for repair, to pour into pots and pans, what he believes is the earthly equivalent of the Nectar of Immortality of The Gods, to which all the respective households would wake up to, to drink- milk.

It is a right he has inherited from the many generations of 'guhals'- milkmen- his family has produced, right from the time they migrated from the Himalayan kingdom. The stamp of being a 'Nepali' guhal, adds authenticity to him and builds his brand.

It is his delivery of milk from his cows that will bring energy and vitality to all the families in Imranpur who have subscribed this service with him. He is held by a sense of tremendous duty which he holds sacred as he goes about making his deliveries. And it is this sense of duty done with utmost care and sincerity that makes him wheel past the gates of the Staff Campus of the Institute of Technical Education, Imranpur and brings him to the B Block, all the way up to the second floor and knock at the doors of the newly arrived residents whom he must take into his fold, so that they too may benefit from the milk of his cows.

****

I had been sleeping fitfully knowing fully well that Sunday morning was no time for me to be up early. Outside, the birds were prancing and chirping about on the window sill and there were sounds of the nearby households waking up. But I waved them off, much like I did the mosquitoes that had bulldozed their way through the gap made by the mosquito net as it untucked from below the mattress and were persistently buzzing over my ears. Slipping my head under the pillow, I continued to sleep.

That is when the door bell rang. It rang half a dozen times more before it succeeded in getting me out of bed through the tangles of the low hanging mosquito net. Opening the door, I found a milk man.

'Warm, fresh milk, bhonti!' he announced. I mumbled amidst yawns that I am allergic to milk. 'Use it to for tea, bhonti!' He advised. More yawns followed and this time I said I like my tea black. 'Payash, bhon-ti?' He offered, the 'ti' syllable twanging in a tone of desperate plea to agree to his offer, as I muttered a Thank You and closing the door, went back to sleep.

It may have been quite some time, but in sleep it only felt like it was a short time when the bell rang again.

'Hi! Mridu here!' A voice greeted me. 'I have joined as a faculty in the Department of Computer Science.'

'Awesome!'

'Yeah!'

I thought that was it, but she didn't leave.

'Errr... Do you have a stool? A high rising one? Actually I just moved in.' I apologized at not having one and finished the conversation to hurry off to sleep.

A few minutes later, the bell rang again. It was Khuri. She had come with a plate of breakfast for me. I managed to smile, thank and take the plate, before shutting the door firmly muttering under my breath. After this, I gave up further attempts to return to sleep. I had been charmed thrice. I could do without any more.

I was right.

Just as I had got ready for the day and was about to sit down for breakfast, Aunt Sarah called up. She sounded pretty excited and in her excitement she was struggling to speak. I wondered what it might be. After long minutes of 'Ashie..you know what, Ashie' going in a seemingly never ending loop, she was finally was able to come to the point.

'Varun', she said. Eh?

'We found your 'The One', Ashie! It is Varun!'

I felt the colour rising in my cheeks.

After having success in obtaining a sweet tempered Goan boy for her Amy and being told by Eddie that he would find his One, when he would indeed find his One, Auntie had decided it was my turn. She was insistent on helping me out in making my choice, while I wondered why I would need help on a matter I was not immediately keen on. Personally I felt that, she was just plain keen to continue her match making skills with our generation as well. After all she was good at it.

She even understood the Assamese mentality of a mere agreement of horoscopes of two strangers, being sufficient to announce an engagement. Though she did get one prepared for herself when she was getting married to Uncle Phukan, she still didn't quite 'get it'. But in her case, she and uncle knew each other through the many occasions of the tea garden life. The horoscope was a mere formality.

Of course, there were protests from the Phukan family. But, Aunt, having developed a genuine liking for the place and its people, had already adopted much of the Assamese way of life. Also, by single handedly cooking and serving the traditional Assamese platter beginning with *khar*, going on to fish in mustard sauce, *masor-tenga* and ending with the sweet tomato gravy *umbol*, she had clinched the match!

There was no scope for further complaints. It was even rumoured that her mother-in-law, who considered herself the best cook in the ever increasing joint family, revealed in private that Aunt was better than her.

In my case, Aunt was hoping that there would be someone from the IT company or thereabouts. Neighbours had given her the impression that if someone went to Bengaluru to study or work, then in nine out of ten cases, they would also find someone to marry from there.

I, however, seemed to be that rare tenth case. Aunt couldn't understand this and I couldn't explain it. Just as I couldn't explain it to Sheyfali, my roommate at the Koramangala flat in Bengaluru, the day I had moved in and she found that I had come by myself.

'Your boyfriend didn't offer to help?' She asked. 'I don't have one.' I replied. She had one, she told me. She had been waiting for me to show up so she could quickly show me around and leave. She had a date planned.

How could there be no one? Aunt wondered too, just like Sheyfali and then went on to decide that some proactive measures were required.

It was not her own land of birth, where young people could keep dating and getting married could be thought of when 'it felt right'. This was India, where, a girl staying unmarried beyond an age was likely to attract unflattering labels like 'Old Maid' and 'Beyond Selling date'. Neither was Guwahati a metro, where the girl could use the '30s is the new 20s' attitude to live her life. There was also my unusual family background adding to it.

So after much brain storming all by herself, on What Type and What Else, she had advertised on the matrimonial pages of the highly reputed The North East Guardian and after sorting through the responses, picked Varun from the category of 'Assamese Cosmopolitan' where caste and religion was no bar.

She had also considered putting up the ad on a couple of national dailies that devoted an eight page weekend supplement devoted to a nationwide search for brides and grooms. But she had been informed by her friends that these came with talk of money and property matters. This being naturally beyond her capacity to understand, she, dropped the idea at once.

'Now, isn't that a very good find?' She exclaimed as she showed me his photo. He certainly did look handsome. I blushed. 'Save those blushes for later, baby!' She teased, making me go more pink. It was for the first time I was looking at a young man with intentions beyond friendship. Intentions that would involve intimacy and sharing. *Sharing*- I frowned.

'What happened?,' enquired Aunt seeing the sudden change of expression. I shook my head forcing a smile as I uttered a weak, 'Nothing'. 'He is a Marketing Manager with a sports channel.' Aunt detailed. 'Sounds good.' I said, not really knowing if it was good indeed. 'He will come next Tuesday evening to take you out for dinner.' This was unexpected. My heart skipped a beat.

There had been the usual rounds of familial discussions that covered an entire spectrum of topics. This was natural. But my Aunt had successfully managed to introduce the 'dating' concept too which was why Varun was to show up to take me out for an evening.

'Is it fine?' Aunt asked me.

'Umm.. Ah, yes.' I mumbled.

'Ok, then I will let him know.'

She went on to give an outline of what she proposed to do to facilitate easy conversations between Varun and me but almost all of that whizzed past my ears. I could feel uncertainty taking me in its grip. May be I was nervous. Or shy. I didn't know. It certainly wasn't a feeling of elation. And it wasn't entirely a scare. But it was definitely there, a feeling that made my heart brake its beating, purse my lips and let my fingers get entwined.

Was it the old fear of being questioned about not being 'firangi' enough rising again? Because, that bullying instance at school had me keep people at a distance, especially boys. What if Varun also asked the same questions? What would I say? Would he understand?

After much thinking on this, I decided that if it had come to this point of meeting me, all these questions must have been dealt with by none other than the skillful Aunt Sarah. Telling myself that these were unfounded fears, I began to focus on what my Tuesday evening would be like.

At times like this, I liked to pull out the family album and pour through it re-living all the good times our family had been through. I especially liked to look with keen eyes at daddy's old photos for the sheer amusement that his old fashioned outfits and accessories offered. When we were young, Eddie, Amy and I would have a field time pointing them out and rolling with laughter. Eddie, who was an expert at passing the cheekiest comments, would make it a point to say his remarks in daddy's hearing purely for the sake of seeing him annoyed.

As I leafed through the pages, I went through photos that showed daddy in his tennis gear ready to hit the court; on a horse, looking every inch the English rider; at a prize distribution for a horticulture show; swimming with his friends while on a picnic during his younger days and eventually I came across one where daddy was the Best Man at his best friend Bill's wedding. On the opposite page was daddy himself at his own wedding.

The wedding photos always puzzled me.

In it, the bride was dressed in *mekhela chador*, complete with her *uroni*, the veil, covering her entire face while the groom was dressed in full suit leaving no doubt that he was a bridegroom from the west.

'What was the point of this photo?' I would always ask in jest causing Eddie to say that the bride was making faces of regret at having to marry a fat nosed, long eared man and so had kept her veil tight. It was a ridiculous explanation. And it got his mother to give him a solid spank which had him shut up.

That evening, I sat with that photo in front of me. Running my hands gently over it, I wondered how long would it be now before I could add one such of my own. And would that really be Varun by my veiled side?

16 GETTING STARTED

'In that case, let us look into the subject allotment for the next semester', suggested Sudhir when I told him that day to day dedicated invigilation was not something I would want to do. I found it very taxing to keep students at bay from their nefarious intentions and mechanisms of cheating. Long bathroom breaks in a pre planned sequence, being an all time favorite.

I wished that I could have said that the girls were better. Not that they weren't. But, as I found, they were better only till they were caught too. Which I did find, when I saw the professor in Mechanical Drawing scolding one, as I walked past the hall the other day.

'I guess we are dealing with an entirely different generation.' I concluded and fell silent. 'Guess so, these ones think that teachers should be their fans, unlike in our times', shared Sudhir and then joined me in my silence.

'So then, let us get back to decide which subject for whom.' He spoke coming back to the original point. 'But I don't know everyone.' I pointed out. 'That's ok. You just tell me what subject you will take up.'

'Ok. What are my choices?' I asked secretly hoping that none of them would be a heavy duty subject. I had dealt with them once in the past as a student and that was all that I could take. I would not be pleased to revisit them again. In the Past is where they should be put.

Sudhir took a pause here, before admitting that while I did have a choice, actually I didn't have one as well. First of all, all except two subjects had already been allotted. A step necessitated by the fact that the professors teaching them would be ones retired from the glorified IIT, Guwahati. Secondly, of the two remaining subjects, Sudhir blushed to confess that, one was being preferred by his fiancée Nandita, currently on leave. In fact, she had already prepared her lesson plans. So that effectively left me with only one subject.
'Which is that?' I asked, fear rising within.

'Electronic Devices', came the reply.

'Which was the other one?'

'Network Theory.'

'I like Electronic Devices.'

'I'll take that', I confirmed feeling relieved that I did not have to deal with a maths intensive subject such as Network Theory. Sudhir also was equally relieved. He had so long been trapped between scheming students and warring professors, that even a minor respite from it was a joy treasured.

I too was feeling happy because now I had something definite to do while at the college. After managing a desktop computer all to myself and gathering all the books on my subject from the library, I sat down to study. There was nothing studious about my method of studying. If at all anything, it could be regarded as frivolous. I would take a fifteen minute break for every fifteen minutes of study. And in those fifteen minutes of break time, I would browse the internet checking my mails from friends I had separated from my old IT world, scrolling through the various updates of people and businesses around the world through their timeline on Facebook, not to mention, freely scouting for history of wars and historical places in the north east or stare out of the window at the mountains.

This caused occasional remarks from Sudhir that it was good to be interested in history and nature. 'It is good to have a hobby'. I smiled politely and took it as an opportunity to ask if I would have the luck of finding a trekking group. 'Well, I don't know of any trekking group but if you went a little further from the Imry Chariali towards Bipul Nagar, on the right side you will find The War Memorial Museum. I have heard it has a few things from the olden times. Lately they discovered some memorials to tea planters who had been active in the many wars. They had got covered amidst bushes, damaged by elephants trampling about and all. So it's mainly that.'

I couldn't believe what I had heard. It looked as if the universe had suddenly put me in the midst of answers. Of course, I was excited. 'Have you been there?' 'No, not really. But I know someone who can help you get there.'

It was the cashier at a nearby eat out called Dunlop Hills. Sudhir went there for his lunch frequently with a few others at the college. He suggested that I went along that afternoon so that he could facilitate the necessary introductions.

So that afternoon, I joined half a dozen of professors from the college in having lunch at Dunlop Hills. At first when I saw the place, I felt like laughing. 'That's what they call a hill?' I could not resist a good natured jeer. It was just ten steps above the road. But when I saw the interiors, I was much impressed. The place was air conditioned and clean; had music playing and the television was on tuned to a news channel- all of that at cheap rates. 'Wow!' I could not help exclaiming.

'It has free wi-fi also', beamed the physics teacher and for the first time I noticed him smiling despite the seal of a doomed teaching fate still fixed on his face. For this new information, I actually had no reaction. All I could think of was having respect for the owner. 'And you are sure he makes profit?' I asked. Someone replied that the owner was already way too rich to bother about it now.

'You will find a lot of our students here when its class time at the college.' Sudhir said unable to suppress a laugh. Such frequent visits made the staff at Dunlop Hills pretty friendly with the students and they had begun offering call-to-order and 'free hostel delivery' services as well. Both parties were on extremely friendly terms, a few even beginning to consider them as family. Especially the ones who ran out of their money quite early in the month or when they needed some secret, extra help like that forbidden bottle that had to be ….

Ah! Guess Sudhir was right about the students expecting us to be their fans.

It was all very interesting and new to me. We ordered the ever popular Assamese dish of 'fish-rice' and proceeded with it. When we were done, Sudhir called me over to the cash counter. 'He's Sarat', he introduced me to the cashier. 'His friend is the curator of that Museum I had spoken of'. I exchanged pleasantries with the fellow whom I found to be quite amiable and requested him to convey to his friend if a visit could be arranged.

Sarat replied that he would be delighted. And anyway, anyone from the college was always welcome. I raised my eyebrows at that and gave a smile.

Back at the college, I felt pretty light in the head and heart so much so that occasionally, I found myself humming songs, gradually merging into the humdrum of the surrounding. Occasionally, a faculty would pass by waving a hello or a more familiar one like Debhargya would walk in to share his latest grief from conducting his classes or Mridu coming by to ask if I wanted to join her for a walk or when I would like to leave.

These were delightful moments that were periodically disturbed by shouts, thuds and other forms of commotion from the Head's office. 'That's our Principal sir annoyed over some matter.' Sudhir informed.

I was a little alarmed and hoped that he kept all of that confined to his room. But that did not always happen. Once, I saw him charging after Minal Borthakur in the corridor telling her to 'get away and leave' because 'that's how much I care about your decisions' and another time we all heard him flying at just about anyone who showed up in his presence.

One day, when I looked up from my computer screen after one of my fifteen minute breaks, I found him staring at me. It was all so sudden and unexpected that I nearly fell off my seat and screamed. But collecting myself together, I greeted him and asked him if there was something I could do for him. He just asked me calmly if I had seen Sudhir anywhere. I hadn't. He merely said an 'Ok' and left.

'He can be quite a tsunami of anger when offended', claimed Sudhir when I told him about it. 'But he's excellent at keeping this place together.'

One month into this institute and I could already see that.

Much like I could also see those tempting mountains that reminded me that I had a visit to them pending. Not to mention that I did have *graves* on my mind.

17 OPENING GOOGLY

Trying to understand the average Ayotic is a brain eater. Though thankfully, following their posts on all possible social media forums simplifies the matter since they are personifications of the various posts on engineering students on Facebook.

The number of 'likes', 'shares' and comments that said 'Tamaam!' on posts that claimed that Only an Engineering Student Can Understand the Value of Studying the Night Before the Exam which was nothing but a photo of a group of insane looking fellows, barely dressed and with bloodshot eyes clinging onto a book as they rushed to the exam hall, proved beyond means that this was actually them.

Then there were others like 'Maggi is best cooked only by an Engineering student' that generated a lot of heated discussion on the quality of food they had to endure at their institute; despite the fact that hostellers universally did a lot of time pass on this very same topic ever since the concept of being a hosteller was introduced by the intellectuals among the masses and who still never could get this mystery of bad food solved.

Among the rest, were the usual suspect of posts that claimed that the engineering student never sleeps at night; an engineering student is always innocent in front of parents; scolding an engineer is like killing the mosquito on your cheek-you slap yourself Ha! Ha!

All of which were in parallel, claimed by students of other subjects in other colleges as well after having made suitable changes, though in separate FB groups to avoid clashes.

The only exception being the ones that declared, Share This Post If You Have Worn Some One Else's Shirt And Gone To Class- Engineering Students Rock!. This had by and large been the punch post of the students of the State run College of Medical Sciences which had somehow leaked out and entered the world of the engineering students leading to mild online skirmishes but otherwise had been okay with everyone.

This was just the high level understanding of a co-ed institution where all interactions, were universally liked, shared, and commented by both the genders. But there was one thing that set the genders apart. It was in the matter of who and what they were 'In a Relationship With' and for how long.

The girls tried to get their boyfriends from the highly desirable Assam State Engineering College(ASEC), failing which they said Yes to boys from IoTE who upon failing to meet their expectations were unceremoniously dumped or put up against 'friends' from ASEC to fight it out. Accordingly, their status on Facebook would change from 'Feeling Excited on Being Single' with no tagging of any friends and a cover photo of herself all decked up, to 'In a Relationship- with ___ You Showed Me the Meaning of Happiness' with the boy friend tagged to it and a profile photo with both of them posing all cuddly-huddly to 'End Of Relationship-Being Single Rocks- Love you girls, mah joys of life..muuaah!!' with all the fellow hostellers and roommates tagged and a group photo of them all as the cover and profile picture as well.

Whereas, the boys tried their luck with the girls from IoTE, failing which they wrote deeply emotional philosophies on their Facebook Walls that invited little or no social attention. Those with a little talent among them would resort to writing songs. This at least got them some attention from girls who generally felt very motherly or sisterly towards such heartbroken cases. For this reason, their Facebook status either read 'In a Complicated relationship' or 'Divorced'.

To be single was unacceptable and to be in a happy committed relationship, rare. Photographs, they had none to share. Except for the occasional nerd who, having made a little progress with his project on the ubiquitous robotic arm, would take a selfie with his monstrous device and post it saying 'With my baby..feeling happy..all thanks to God and my parents'. Once in a while, a professor might also get named in the post. And for all that effort, he would get a handful of comments like,

'Awesome, brother!'

'Kya baat, bhai!'

'DUDE, man!'

Those who had made a choice of challenging this fate, often found themselves facing hurly-burly overgrown boys in undersized clothing with a general appearance of being Early Man Dressed in faded and torn Lee Cooper, at lonely unlit intersections of roads, who had a knack of sending them flying in mid air only to land as an 'In Patient' in the village's only hospital. They would no doubt have learnt the lesson upon their discharge, albeit at the cost of weaker eyesight or a wobbling jaw. Or something else equally disgusting.

But irrespective of all these, the last thing on the average Ayotic's mind has always been, well, being in IoTE which was well demonstrated by the absence recorded in the Attendance Registers. This was clearly a cause of concern and matter of loss in pride for the Head. After all which Head of an Institution would feel proud of being the Head of an Institute where the students didn't come to attend classes? So during the pre semester meet of all the teaching hands, he stated that we all were to take strict measures on this- whatever seemed appropriate to us.

Among the other things that were discussed was the various study programs that would be introduced to the students so that by the time they graduated they would not be mere talking versions of the books and notes that they had read in the class room. Instead, they would have sound practical knowledge. This was by and large received with a lot of appreciative claps and nods and afterwards we dispersed for tea where all the new faculty members were formally introduced.

We were not many of us, just three – Mridu, I and a chap in the Department of Mechanical Engineering but I being the only one in the Department of Electronics & Communication Engineering (E&CE) and the Department having a reputation of being the realm of intelligent beings, attracted the attention of all the retired professors from IIT Guwahati who had been assorted to teach the Ayotics.

From the very beginning, they were unanimous on the point that I did not have a Ph.D. Not that the point missed me. But making a note of it seemed to give them a sense of satisfaction over their credentials and aroused their curiosities. Now, what kind of an Assistant Professor in E&CE did not have a Ph.D in E&CE? They asked one another, as they towered over my five foot three frame. In all probability, my kind.

The next point on which their unity grew unabashedly was the question on *when* would I start my Ph.D. I confessed that I had not even started thinking on that and on the inside, I was beginning to get angry with Daddy Brendon for all having fed all that engineering diversity on me. 'See, what it has got me into?' I was telling him.

Annoyed and irritated, I picked up my cup of coffee and sat down in a corner of the hall. From here, I could hear other conversations of a different nature. Hiramoni ma'am, together with Madhobi ma'am and Mridu were discussing, rather, dissecting their private lives with the other women teachers.

Madhobi ma'am was quite voluble, never seeming to want to stop. She had a lot to say about her life on every topic being brought up. Currently, Mridu's engagement had taken her focus. Now, this was definitely a topic on which Madhobi ma'am seemed to have really much to say since she herself had got married recently. Motivated by this development, she declared that Mridu should learn from her since, after all she had bagged not only the Most Desirable Husband but also a Most Desirable Mother in-law, a Most Desirable House, a Most Desirable Others in-law….when she was rudely interrupted by

Mridu who asked if she also had an equally never ending list of Most Desirable Desires. This invited polite giggles from the other teachers assembled, including Hiramoni ma'am but it was clear to all that the maths teacher did not take kindly to it at all. It was also likely that she had taken this very personally.

'Ashima!' I heard Nandita, Sudhir's fiancée's voice. She was back now from her leave. Searching for me in the crowd and finding me here, she came over and sat down next to me.

'It's ok, dear', she said giving me a friendly squeeze on my shoulder. 'Don't take it so personally. They are like that.' She was, of course referring to the remarks made by the faculty from our stream on my academic capacity, a short while back. She had developed this depth of maturity by having repeatedly heard from them that while their mere presence in an IIT classroom caused students to attain instant enlightment on the subject, here in IoTE, in addition to their presence, even actions like talking, dictating notes, writing on the board and showing slides failed to register any interest in the students.

Given such passionate comparisons that they were capable of, I seemed to have got away lightly with my Ph.D –lessness. So, I took Nandita's advice and decided to ignore them.

Besides, I had a developed a very good lesson plan and devised a good regime that I knew would make my life easy. I owed this confidence to the unbelievingly simple and super elegant Newton's Third Law. On the opening slide deck of each of my lessons, I put one slide on Class Etiquettes on which I had written in bold fonts- Follow Newton's Third Law At All Times For Things Related To This Subject.

Armed with this, I made my way, on the opening day of the semester to the second floor of the East Wing of Education Block Room number 2 where I was to find the class of third semester Electrical Engineering. What I found was an empty classroom full of desks and benches. I waited for full five minutes tapping my fingers against the book I was carrying and then, returning to the Dr. B.N. Saikia lab, pulled out the register and marked 'Ab' against 60 names. I repeated this exercise for the next two days as well, gradually developing a belief that it was not a Ph D that qualified one as an Assistant Professor but the amount of patience one could have in waiting for potential students to show up. Maybe I could do a Ph D on showing the correlation on *that*. Hah!

Finally, on the fourth day, I was blessed with the presence of twenty students whose excitement on seeing me turned to amusement when I showed them my slide on Class Etiquettes. By the post lunch lab session only two of them could remember what had been taught in the second semester thereby causing me to send the rest to the library for a short study.

Then, two weeks later, according to my session plan, I conducted an open book test of five multiple choice questions. I allowed free consultation with friends. But when even this could not get the students the stellar performance they had been expecting of themselves, I knew that I had zapped some amount of their 'enzoiment'.

But I was more bothered with having put my regime in place with the Newtonian law as my guiding force. That's what mattered to me. For now, I could think seriously of visiting the War Memorial Museum and who knows, the mountains too.

18 INSECURE SECURITY

Hazarika was never known for being duty bound. He had a conscience that belonged to another world of dutifulness. Many a well wisher of Ayote had reported to the Head of Administration that he was not a right pick for the job. For, they had seen him talking to the wind and singing to stray cows. 'Haza is always having mazza', is how they talked about him.

The latest episode being, the unnatural and unexpected appearance of the latest model of a Bajaj Pulsar bike at the back of the boys' hostel haphazardly hidden amidst the bushes, despite there being a security guard deputed at the gate of the hostel to prevent this kind of a surprise. That day, this Guard was supposed to manifest itself in the form of an alert Hazarika but obviously had not. It had instead manifested itself under the shade of the nearby grove of trees and gone to sleep with a newspaper over his face.

'May be that's when the bike came in.' He informed everyone when quizzed on the matter. When someone took the trouble of explaining to him that a bike did not possess free will that could make it come in on its own, he pleaded his lack of intelligence on the matter. 'As if he ever had any!' The Admin threw a taunt and asked the Hostel Management to dismiss him immediately, which, of course they refused on grounds of no 'solid evidence.'

The closest evidence that could be gathered was clicking him as he snored away to glory when he should have been on a strict watch.

This was dismissed by the Admin which said that they had actually seen in person, the whole lot of security staff fast asleep when they should have been on an especially strict watch. So, Hazarika *alone* could not be punished.

With that, the intensity with which the interested public highlighted Haza's shortcomings had come down. Nevertheless, sporadic incidents establishing the very same would manage to make itself appear and reappear over and again.

Once, under his non vigilant eyes, a fellow from the hostel had managed to break out, run into the territory of a neighbouring house, settle a score with the sleeping residents and jump back into his room. When the affected party turned up with an arm of the law for support to make a point, both the boy and the guard denied the incident.

'Blasphemy!', declared the neighbour. 'How can you say such a thing?'

The Admin said that they could. That's why they had.

'Huh?'

Well, the guard never saw him leave or return. Neither does the boy admit it. So that's that.

'You mean to say that we hallucinated the whole thing?'

Given that it had happened in the aftermath of the Great Imry Village Lucky Dip, the Admin couldn't say 'No' for sure. For, the event was known to have produced many an unexpected and undesirable result on the villagers; hallucination being one of them.

This created a lot of bad blood between Ayote and the neighbours; the neighbours and the police and finally, the police and Ayote. A side effect of this was that both Haza and the boy were let off with a strict warning, the violation of which would attract harsh terms.

Shortly after this, a group of fishing women arrived at the doorsteps of the Admin determined to beat up Hazarika with the ends of their *mekhela* if they were denied justice on the issue of Haza selling illegitimate fish. The Admin found this to be a very interesting issue. To begin with, how did one figure out the legitimacy of the fish?

'It is simple', said one of the fishing women. If it was from a water body and bought from them, then it was legitimate! Very simple, admitted the Admin. In that case, was Haza buying fish from them and selling it to others. Because Haza was not a water body and therefore his act was pretty illegitimate.

'No', replied another of those women. The Admin was perplexed. Could they explain, please? They told the Admin that he was keeping fish in the pits dug for construction of the proposed swimming pool and selling them. They wanted to know why the college encouraged it.

The college didn't, declared the Admin and sent for Haza.

Haza arrived exasperated. He swore by the canteen staff that all the fish in those pits were because of the rains that had caused the fishes to get washed off from the adjacent rice fields. It was 'fish erosion'. These were the fishes that he was selling. When called upon to confirm this, the canteen staff felt like it was fishing in troubled waters and therefore did not respond.

Given that this had happened in the aftermath of the heavy rains and heavy rains were known to have such effects on fields and fishes, the Admin couldn't take a decision. Whereupon, yet another of the women pointed out that this was misuse of college property. These sounded like educated words. The Admin fined ninety percent of Haza's earnings from the fishes and sent home the fishing women.

'Can't you be a little responsible?', asked the Admin of Haza.

'But I am!' He responded.

The Admin was taken aback but did not risk asking, 'How So?' They would give him one last chance by entrusting him with the maintenance of the Roll Call Register. The slightest of discrepancies and out he would go. Haza remained silent to show his agreement.

Haza wasn't sure if he was upset about the new assignment. The boys were always on the lookout for passing unflattering comments. Yes, they were always doing that. But now, they would do it even more because of the increase in the number of interactions with him- two roll calls every day, seven days of the week, week after week, month after month, till end of semester, definitely.

Ah! What joys! (For the boys)

But lo, what irritations! (For Haza)

It made the roll calling difficult. The voices were forever disguised or muffled or squeaky or shrill but never in their original form. Except in room number 304. How he wished the other boys had learnt manners from the ones in 304!

'What will become of me?', moaned Hazarika to his friend Sarat, when he met him in the evening. Sarat didn't know what to say. Personally, he felt that whatever fate settled on Hazarika, it could not be worse than what Sarat himself had to bear with- a set of seven motherless children, a pair of elderly parents and a set of extremely old grandparents, all catered to, by his earnings alone. Hazarika on the other hand, had no such worries. He was one of the many forsaken members of his ever growing joint family that always seemed to have the basic provision of food and shelter made available for this category of family members. So, in a way, he doing any kind of job that gave him any kind of pay was a bonus.

Sarat and Hazarika had been childhood friends. Each knew well what the other was capable of and not. There was no hiding anything. And friendship demanded the offer of welfare to everyone involved in this relationship.

'You ignore them. Just do your job.' Sarat suggested to Hazarika. 'You think that will work?' He asked. Sarat, being the more intelligent of the two, knew that it was the only thing to do. The real question was whether his friend could do it or not. However, not wanting to put it so bluntly, he just said, 'Try, you can do it'.

Haza felt a little encouraged. In times like these, he had always turned to Sarat for advice. Whenever the going got tough for him, he met Sarat at the Dunlop Hill Restaurant where he was the cashier and got suitable guidance from him. But their meetings were not always of this counseling nature. They also met on other days, even when there wasn't much to talk about. They would meet like two good old friends, discussing the good old times.

It was during one of these meetings that Haza brought up the interesting case of the talented boy at the hostel. The reason Haza had noticed this boy was because he was the only one who didn't mock at him during the roll calls. He was one of the two boys in room 304. The boy never spoke to him but Haza had seen him act at the Inter Departmental gathering, heard him mouth dialogues and instantly was impressed! He had heard him sing as well…though that was in the middle of the night…at another boy's room, where many other boys were present also…this boy had cried, though Haza could not understand what for.

Incidentally, Haza's narration of the boy left an impression on Sarat's mind as well. Especially since Haza had told him that the boy could act as well as sing. Now that was something. Not everybody could do that. In the entire village there was only one person who was known to have both these talents and that was Rubul Kalita. This is what made Rubul stand out from the rest of the actors. It had made him special. But now he was gone. Sarat made up his mind to ask Haza more about this boy at a later time when it would be more likely to have a productive conversation with him. Till then, the most that he could do was share this impression with Anil Thikedar. This, he did, on the day the Thikedar's most prized actor- Rubul Kalita- had resigned from his establishment. The Thikedar had smiled at this piece of information and nodded, muttering 'Besides, which boy didn't want help with money these days?'

19 ONE HELL OF PROGRESS

It was as usual a pleasant Saturday afternoon and to make it even more pleasant, I was spending it at the Dunlop Hill Restaurant browsing the free internet, trying to set fresh fire to the trail of the long lost Mr. Bharadwaj. I must confess, I was not at all having a rewarding experience. My first focus was, of course, the lake from which no return was possible, at least as per my late Uncle's letter. When I started my search, I was expecting a lot of tales on mysterious disappearances caused by this piece of water body. So I was really surprised when it turned out that all this talk about the lake was a mere figment of historic imagination.

Not the lake though. It did exist along the Assam Myanmar border near the Pangsau Pass and it turned out to be a popular tourist spot too. I saw photos of people enjoying rides on its serene waters on many websites and blogs by biking adventurers' talking of it. And sure enough, they all had returned from it safe and sound. So why is it that my father and his fellow mates, if any, did not? I had a hunch it had less to do with the lake itself.

But all this I had discovered before arriving at Imry, while I was still at my old job. It was at this point of search that I had taken a break by socializing online and thereafter, went down in the eyes of my employer as well as the history of the company pay roll.

There was 'something else' that I had not come across yet. It had to do with my hunch about the lake. A little more reading revealed that I was right in my thinking. It turned out that all this hoopla of the lake sucking in visitors was all but a hypothesis someone had come up with to justify why planes had not safely landed and soldiers could not make progress towards the enemy, during the war. Because, post the war, tourist activities in and around the lake began flourishing and there seemed to be no trace of any mishaps initiated by the lake on the visitors. Hah!

So my father had actually been a victim of unwarranted hypothesis rather than facts. But at least I got a hint as to who he might have been- a soldier. The only people who had any reason to go anywhere near that lake, in the 1940s, had to be a soldier. There was no other reason for them to be there. That was pretty good a finding for me, for then. For one evening this was a good achievement.

I continued reading, feeling quite enthralled, what with one link of a page leading me to another and in the process realizing new things. Like the existence of the 'Hell Gate' that would lead to the 'Hell Pass', for instance. The Hell Gate was a check post marking the entry to the historic and strategic Stiltwell Road running past the village of Ledu in Assam that led to the Pangsau Pass in Myanmar where this lake of enormous notoriety sat.

In the past, soldiers had labored their way through the snaky path on the Pass when moving from Burma through India, to Kunming in China while traversing the Patkai range. It was the scene of action for the Second World War. With the severest of hairpin turns one could have on a mountain and a route infested with mosquitoes, wild animals, swamps and given at the time of war- the enemy, it stood as the mother of all war fare challenges in such terrain. Pangsau Pass had rightfully earned itself the nickname of being the Hell Pass, complete with a check post to guide it.

To climb through this stretch of a road and come out unscathed by the wily attacking means of the enemy or without picking up life threatening diseases after being bit by mosquitoes was considered nothing short of a miracle. Only that, there were not many who had this miracle working for them. Most fell ill and many fell to the sudden attacks of the enemy. The remaining surviving ones barely managed to cross the road and arrive with a little life remaining in them. I could now gauge the 'hellishness' of this pass.

What was most interesting about this whole affair at the Hell Pass was that the fallen soldiers were not allowed to be forgotten just like that. A quick prayer and short ritual for each of them was arranged for and they were buried in a hastily pulled up burial ground. Of course, there were times when a soldier had to be laid to rest along the way too. So, the latter half of the Pass or rather, the road closer to the Lake, got dotted with many single graves.

I had a feeling that, assuming that Mr. Bharadwaj was indeed a soldier, then he had been making his way in this pass. So then, either he crossed it to reach the lake or he did not. Given what I had read in my step dad's letter, I felt that this is what he had been trying to mean. That made sense. Besides, I now had a clear idea of what I should do, if I want to visit my Father- go visit this place and spot his grave.

A moment later, I realized the folly of this deduction. If my theory was correct, then I should have been celebrating my seventieth birthday and been leading a retired life with grandchildren. Instead, I only had blown off less than half that number of candles on my last birthday.

Though discouraged by the confusion, I still felt determined to go ahead and read more. I badly wanted to crack this. But then mental fatigue started to set in and then there were four other people in the hall with me who were talking loudly and disturbing me. This did not agree with me.

I like to work in quietness. Dunlop Hill is normally deserted on weekend afternoons which is why I had opted to go there. I tried 'ssh-ssh-ing' them for a while but it didn't help much. So, I decided it was best to wrap up for the day. As I left Dunlop Hill, I didn't intend to over hear any conversations but at the same time, words did reach my ears and I got shots of conversations in to my hearing.

'Done!!!'

'You sure?'

'Of course! Been waiting for this!'

'Your life depends on it.'

'Ah, don't think so.'

'All worked out?'

'Yaay!'

'Money no problem?'

'No problem!'

'Hurray!!!'

One of them I recognized as Sarat, the cashier of Dunlop Hill. The other, a rather portly and richly dressed figure with a business like look on his face might have been the owner of Dunlop. For he seemed to match whatever I had heard of him. The other two appeared to be two teenage boys. One wore red and black floaters with matching red and black tee and shorts. While the other looked satisfied that he had finally taken up his responsibility towards himself. Both high- five-ed with each other.

20 THE INSPECTOR

The Imranpur Police Station (Port Side), stood removed from the rush of the main village life. It was surrounded by laziness well provided by the young goat-lings grazing off its grounds and puplings knocking down each other as they rolled about. There was not much to give the police station a sense of its being or a reason to exist. It was only a collection of dilapidated buildings and the worn out look reflected the current state of affairs. Within, the indolence was well supported by rows of pencil sketches of prospective jail inmates that were pasted on the walls.

Amidst it all, sat Inspector Saikia having had enough of his job.

In all honesty, he had begun to doubt what his job actually was about. Was it to crack crimes that besieged Imranpur or try his hand at unrevealing secrets of the village? To Saikia, it did not feel like the former. So his feeling had more to do with being irritated. Irritation on why people could not be open and straightforward about the secrets which were anyway not worth keeping? He felt even more irritated when these folks knew who or/and what the secret was. It felt as if they were being paid to keep the secret.

For instance, those 'would be' jail inmates.

No one had seen them but many had described them. No one knew the exact nature of their crime but each had many credited to their name. The inspector wondered if it would ever come to seeing them eye to eye, let alone arresting them. He had no leads to work on and only descriptions to follow on. Certainly, one could not arrest a 'description'. That just about sealed the deal on his success rate as an Inspector which did not show any indications of becoming better. Not at this rate, he had concluded.

He looked back and thought of his days at the State Police Academy. How ambitious he had been! No doubt a rising star.

In fact, he had believed that he was going to have a herculean impact on the crime scene of the state. How was he to know that Fate had something else in mind for him. He did find it out, of course, when upon graduation from the Academy, it was to a village that he had to proceed. Even so, he hadn't given up his dreams and hopes. Saikia's aspirations were not meant for being buried so soon and in such a lame fashion.

He sought the positive in the situation. He began with the first thought that, some of the more challenging crimes had occurred in the villages. What was the truth of this impression, one couldn't say but he certainly seemed convinced by it. Wasn't it so?, he reasoned to himself. He had read a lot of books where this was the case. Especially the one about an elderly spinster who lived in St Mary Mead and was seemingly only knitting but all the while knew all about the murders happening around. A world famous Agatha Somebody had written about her. So surely, it could not have been a fabrication of his imagination, however non fertile it was.

For days he waited at his desk looking with expectant eyes at the veiled women passing by; hoping that one of them would drop in to seek his intervention in a seemingly simple affair that would eventually turn out to be something of a thriller. Unfortunately, by Sherlock, only the elementaries prevailed, like stolen cycle rickshaws, fights over unsettled bills, misrepresentation of farm animals etc. Well, naturally it was a disappointment. But Saikia was not about to give up just then. A glimmer of new hope had arisen when it was announced that a new engineering college was to be opened soon in the village.

When the technical institute had become fully functional, it looked as if it might provide a breather to his dampened hopes. Not that technical institutes are hot beds of crime. But in a village like Imranpur, where exchange of consumer durables was in itself a perplexing affair, the existence of a technical establishment was posed to be regarded as an enigma. That, in itself was sufficient to trigger the wrong. However, apart from being unnecessarily pulled in by some residents on the perplexing case of locked-college boy-slapping-sleeping residents- only to have had the case dismissed, the institute did nothing to utilize his skills.

By the college authority 'utilizing his skills', what Saikia had in mind was trying to do something big. Like, controlling a huge agitating crowd. Something like, students agitating on a mass level. He remembered an uncle in the family who, as a student had participated in the Oil Refinery Agitation of '57. Of course, at that time all the elders of the house had severely reprimanded him for wasting his time in this manner. But when the refinery eventually came about in '62 and the uncle managed to get a job in it, the same people acknowledged him as a hero.

Saikia was also able to recollect a great- great grandfather who had been part of the earliest known student movement in the history of Assam. The demands of this movement had resulted in the establishment of the highly reputed Cotton College of present day, where Saikia himself had the opportunity to study. Of whether or not his agitating ancestor had also got the same chance, no one in the family seemed to remember. They generally believed it to be so.

Reflecting at this constructive effect that the student movements had on his life and family, Saikia realized that he would be filled with guilt if he had to police them. Yet he could not shake off the feeling that only a student agitation could rescue him from his current state of unsuitable work. There remained no doubt that he was disappointed with the way things were posed at his work.

Sometimes, he thought of his counterpart at the Imranpur Police Station (City Side) and wondered if it was any better. Even though he had heard that the cases on the Port Side is always greener in terms of arrests made.

Saikia's only consolation was that he had a *bomblast-ic* start to his career. Blasts.

Bombs going off every now and then. There was no anticipating when, where and other details like that about them. There used to be a time when one was assured of at least one blast a day, anywhere. Being prepared was the key. Nothing else helped. Especially for Saikia who was hit by a bomb, on three consecutive instances while on duty. Each time, each of the bombs hit him while he was in the same beat location.

It was too much of a coincidence because, each time the dispenser of the bombs was a different antisocial outfit. What common grievance each of them nursed against Saikia that resulted in this action defied his intelligence. Even the local media regarded it with curiosity.

Initially, they reported it as a food for social thinking. However, as days passed by and after Saikia was featured in the interview columns of the local dailies and the TV channels, it only ended up getting spiced. But to the highly haggled Saikia, what was surprising was that it was not the same bomb that was repeating itself. Of course, apart from Saikia, no one else seemed perturbed by this. It did not even have a humorous appeal.

He sighed heavily. It was time for another beat round.

'Sir!' cried a voice as he got up from his chair.

A middle aged woman sobbing uncontrollably was standing with her twenty something son at the door. 'Sir!', called the boy again.

'Yes?'

'We have come to file a report, sir!'

'Okay.'

It was clear that Saikia was not thrilled at the prospect of report writing just then. Actually, he was a little suspicious about it. The last time he had to file a report, it was for a missing cow.

'I love my cow!' The owner of the cow had cried. Apparently, many more villagers were in love with the same cow and one of them seemed to have had the courage to elope with it as well. Saikia had lost it completely, then. This was the limits in having his bare minimum expectations from the job getting fractured mercilessly. Of all the evils that could be, it had come down to a missing cow!

A missing cow!

He was sure nobody could beat that. A missing cow!

'Yes?' He asked weakly trying to recover himself from the remembrances of the cow episode.

'A report, sir', pleaded the boy between his tears. 'My father has been missing since three days, sir!' He said. At this, the mother broke into another round of sobs, burying her face onto the ends of her *chador.*

Saikia sat up straight now. This, he noted, is good. It was about humans. Not only that, it was about missing humans. Surely, this ought to be more thrilling than missing cows. 'Now, now', began Saikia getting into his inspectorial mode. 'Give me the details. Name?'

'Rubul Kalita'

Saikia was startled.

'You don't mean Rubul Kalita, the theater actor?'

'That's him', agreed the boy. Wow, Saikia told himself. His luck seemed to be changing for the better. He couldn't believe it. 'Tell me about it.' He said aloud. It was probably for the first time since his Academy days that Inspector Saikia felt that he was indeed set to work as an inspector.

21 WHEN THOUGHTS MADE THE MAN

The hazards associated with incomplete education are well known. What is not, is its side effects en route to those hazardous outcomes. At Imry, there were a good number of such souls who had dissociated their paths from education and floated around with little to do. Bikash Kumar was one of them. In fact, he was the ring leader of them all. He had tried his brains at clearing the Matriculation Exam twice and when it had not worked, never bothered with it again. His close friends had ceased such academic pursuits years earlier. It was by virtue of this that he had emerged more learned than them and subsequently, the leader. However, there was a line of difference between the leader and the followers.

The friends had found some means or the other to keep themselves funded- a tea stall here, a little driving there, some shop keeping somewhere else etc. Bikash, on the other hand was not prepared to spare his seemingly better-on-paper intellect over such trivial jobs. He was on the lookout for something that would arouse and maintain his intellectual curiosity. Till date, he had found none so suitable and therefore remained a loiterer. And so in staying funded, he had to depend on his friends.

Recently however, he managed to step up his interest in the managing of Imry's only computer café'- a certain Hari Om Intarnate Cafe- and eventually got employed with it. Initially, the motivation to take up the employment had more to do with getting away from the burdensome everyday shouts of, 'Boy, go, find and do some work, boy!' by his family members. But later, when he started to discover how his intellect was going to be used in this job, he became committed to it. He could look up any website, create and use mail ids for anybody (he made sure that he first got one for himself), book tickets and take their printouts. Now, this was intellectual stuff and he loved it!

The pay wasn't good and he certainly did not have anything in physical form to show off as did his cousin who worked as a security guard for various companies in the city. Now, *he* had lots to show off, indeed. His uniform, for one thing. Among others, there were the photos of himself with the posh company campus as the background and exciting tales of his duties whenever there was an important visit to the company. All this when he wasn't even as educated as Bikash!

Neither was he the only one in the family to take up the job of a Security Guard. There was another cousin who was employed in the security forces of the village's only engineering college.

But this guy and the others including Bikash himself, weren't important to the family. What mattered was that this one had become the most progressive of the family- he was their darling. Of course Bikash did not like it. But he loathed only one of them- the progressive one. The other, he didn't bother with. He disregarded him just like the other members of his family. 'Haza is always having Maza' is what they had to say about him, just as everyone else who knew Haza.

But with respect to the first one, Bikash was quite determined that he was going to break all this hoopla. He would certainly breech this security- he had been picking up a few new technical terms from the new found friends at his work place. 'Hacking', he noted mentally was the correct term. Bikash decided that all that security nonsense had to stop. How- was the question. He needed some time to think.

Thoughts have a habit to coming to Bikash pretty effortlessly. But only idle ones. For the really good ones, he had to exercise his intellect. That is where he was different from the others. With them, either they didn't think or what they thought was useless. Bikash could, on the other hand will his way through the thoughts.

He had been thinking all day and subsequently had collected a few thoughts. There was no sequence to it, though. But he felt that could wait. First of all, he needed matter, substance. Now, at the end of the day, he felt what he had to be enough. They just needed that 'sorting out' to be done. Since he had not pursued a systematic approach, this proved to be a challenging task. He struggled. However, a few days later, at night, as he lay on his bed staring at the stars above, all the assorted thoughts fell into place. A picture emerged. The idea finally footed itself firmly.

He sat up and getting hold of a pen and sheets of paper, started putting into words, The Plan. But before that, first, he had to put down the planning.

1. 1 to get car

2. 1 to drive car

3. 1 to get Gift

4. 1 to unpack Gift

5. 1 to pick Return Gift

6. 1 to deal with Return Gift

7. 1 to return Return Gift

8. Others: 1-2 extras to assist

It was a long list.

Bikash checked to see if it could be reduced. After some thoughts, he rewrote it.

1. 1 to get car and use car

2. 1 to get Gift and unpack Gift

3. 1 to get Return Gift and return Return Gift

4. Others: Me to assist.

That looked much better. Bikash grew confident by the moment. Wait, what if he re-wrote that?

1. 1 to get car and use car

2. 1 to get Gift and unpack Gift & same 1 to get Return Gift and return Return Gift

3. Others: Me to assist.

Now, *that* was way much better.

All he now had to do was find the 'Gift' which also would be the 'Return Gift'. That would need some more thinking. Meanwhile, he decided to arrange for the rest.

22 TUESDAY

Daily late night Skype calls with Eddie, Amy or Aunt Sarah over 'Varun Coming to Meet Ashie on Tuesday' and calls from Sheyfali who was insistent on 'coaching' me for the meeting, had ensured that I slept late and woke up late too. As a habit oriented person, I didn't like it. But it could not be undone.

On Monday evening, Aunt called as expected. As per her earlier plan she would be coming sometime late on Monday evening or sometime during the day on Tuesday so that she could oversee the meeting. 'Ashie', she said as I took her call. Her voice was cold, totally devoid of any excitement. 'Yes Auntie, all well?'

'Ashie-'

'Yes?'

'Varun will not come tomorrow, Ashie.'

She said trying not to sound panicked by this sudden change in plan. 'Ok, so when does he want to come?' I asked trying equally hard to not get distressed by this unexpected news. 'He doesn't want to come at all, Ashie.' This was totally out of the blue.

'Any reason?' I asked.

'The family found something wrong with the horoscope.' Aunt Sarah tried to be as calm as possible when she said this.

'But…' I began but the words would not come. Was this the meaning of being 'Cosmopolitan'? I wondered as a cocktail of sadness, disappointment and anger started building up inside me.

'There will be another one, Ashie. Don't be sad.'

It was hard not to be sad. After days of heart-in-the-sleeves texts and calls, confessing how badly he wanted the days to go by to bring in the Tuesday, suddenly he realized that he didn't have the consent of some of the planets. How convenient!

This was not a good Monday to start the week with.

I climbed up to the terrace of the B Block Flats, watching the sun go down behind mountains. A mild chill filled the air as darkness descended. It felt very gloomy. As if these were the last few moments before the approach of doom and having received heart breaking news only made matters worse. Shortly, the skies came alive with stars and the moon rose. I had to admit that under such skies, both the college and staff campuses looked very impressive.

But however hard I tried that evening to feel cheered by looking at the beautiful night skies, something about them left me feeling as being the least sociable and the loneliest creature in the universe at the moment.

I had the photo album with me. I flipped to the page that had my parents wedding photo. But that day as I looked at that photo, instead of laughing as usual, I was overcome by a sudden fear. What if I never had one such moment in my life? Was it in the stars or was it something else?

23 A PLAY OF TIME

It was seven in the evening when I found myself standing in front of the mirror, looking at the reflection.

'Hi, Ashima!' it greeted me. I responded with a weak 'Hi'. 'Who are you?' I asked it. 'You don't know me?' It asked. I didn't know.

What I saw was the image of a girl dressed in an off white frock of lace, with a string of pearls around her neck, matching ear studs and bracelet. Her eyes were marked out by a fine black line, as if it were marking out a boundary for the emotions in those eyes so that they would not flow beyond it, lest they turned enchanting; while her mild rosy lips seemed to be waiting to break into a warm smile.

'I am waiting for the time to come, for the bell to ring.' It said, adjusting the curls that were settled on her shoulders. 'Tell me, am I looking ok?' She asked. Something about that question snapped me. 'That bell won't ring.' I told her in a harsh tone. 'No time will come and no one will come', this came out in a thunder. 'And you… are looking like a witch!' I declared amidst angry pants. Then, I gave her a hard push away from me.

She let out a shout of being hurt, which made me give her a sound slap. This, she took even more badly, starting to cry softly and then, she seemed to fade…gradually at first, then becoming a blur before finally dissolving into tears that ran down my cheeks.

I walked unsteadily away from the mirror, across the room toward my bed where I buried my face into the pillow and had a little sob. I was supposed to get ready to go for watching a play in the village, not do a mock enactment of dressing up for a date that was never going to happen. How planetary alignments could rapidly alter the scheme of things!

'There will be someone else, soon dear.' Aunt had consoled. At that time, the words did seem to have its intended effect on me. But then, just as I was walking back from the college, I began to wonder about the emotions that I was supposed to feel that day. Emotions that the planets had decided to snatch away from me at the last moment. By the time I reached my quarters, I couldn't help rushing to my wardrobe and taking out the frock which my Aunt had so lovingly chosen for me. I longed to know what it had held for me, which I could not get now.

Did I feel cheated by that reflection in the mirror or was I plain jealous of her? I didn't know. And now, after much crying I didn't seem to have the strength to want to know either. Putting away the jewellery and changing into my usual wear, I splashed up my face with water, letting and hoping that its coolness would wipe away the last hour.

It was now half past seven. I should have been on my way. Before leaving, I checked at the mirror again. This time, I saw myself. Relieved, I grabbed the house key from its stand and shutting the door locked, went out.

24 MAHARANI THEATRES

After being denied a drop on the bike of her squint eyed son at the last minute, Khuri was furious. But soon she realized that this was no time for sulking and that she had to now get into her organizing mode. Her resourcefulness and social networking skills, from which even Zucky could learn a thing or two, rescued her and soon there was a cycle rickshaw on its way to pick us up.

'I will get dressed and come.' She said walking hurriedly into her room. Just as she was about to enter, she turned around and gave me an admiring look. 'You have a nice figure.' She said making my cheeks flush at the unexpected remark. I was in, 'long pants' in Khuri's parlance. The word 'trousers' had not yet entered the vocabulary of the paltry English spoken by the Imranpurites.

My dress code was in accordance with her directions when she still believed that her son would be riding us to the play, with her sitting side saddled behind her son and me sitting normal saddled, behind her. What passers-by would have to say to this, she didn't bother with. But perhaps it had bothered her offspring which is why he had chopped the plan at the last minute and instead, opted to ride off with his own friend in tow.

I had no plans of going play watching but I wanted to keep my mind off the original intentions of the evening. Seeing the advert of the ongoing village theatre, I thought to give it a try and under the circumstances, I decided that Khuri would be the best companion, her antics guaranteed to keep my mind distracted for the rest of the evening. I was right.

By the time she was ready, the rickshaw had also arrived. The rickshaw-wallah, in keeping with the naming nomenclature of other members of his trade, was named after God. In his case, the God was, Kisno.

'O Kisno, you have come with your chariot, is it?' Khuri greeted him as she emerged from the house. The fellow grinned. Apart from his name, he was also a confirmed representative of his profession in terms of his physique. A stick thin guy, I wondered how he was going to manage cycling a heavy weight like Khuri, in whose comparison, I was weightless.

'Your wheels are well aired, hah?' She asked as she struggled to haul herself up the rickshaw. 'Don't be worrying, Khuri. All the tyres are fine', assured Kisno. 'It better be, what with you ferrying your gopis all around, all day. Within the next one minute, we should not be hearing fiss-fiss coming from here and there.'

'I am old for any gopis, O Khuri!'

'Oh, Ai! Hear him!' Khuri said in a mock wail to show her disagreement on the matter.

All settled now, Kisno began his arduous task of pedaling his machine, getting stuck at every speed breaker and pot hole. Though Khuri did not seem to be affected every time the rickshaw bumped its way through them, it did jerk me severely, causing Khuri to come to my rescue by putting her hand around my waist and pulling me towards her. 'Nice curves, girl', she whispered to my growing discomfort. Now I knew why I felt there was something odd about her, the first time I had met her.

In another five minutes, we reached the venue of the play. It was a warm night, with rains being delayed and the effects of this showed on everyone around. Khuri and I were fanning ourselves with our little handkerchiefs and mopping the sweat almost non-stop. Though, it was Kisno who actually took the brunt of it. His physical efforts caused sweat to flood through his being drenching his shirt along except where his sleeveless inner vest tried to stop it. It made him appear like a butterfly of human size proportion.

'Look at him!' Khuri cried feeling amused as the sweat drenched Kisno and I helped her climb down the rickshaw. 'This is what happens, Kisno, when you play too much with your gopis. Look, no energy now!'

Kisno was in no mood to humour her, by now. He too had planned to watch the play and had come dressed in his best available garments. He could very well do without this jibe. 'You come back here at around eleven.' Khuri instructed him as she paid the fare.

The scene at the Maharani Theaters, a large tent, appeared as if a carnival was in progress. It had everything from Ferris wheel, merry-go-rounds to chowmein-n-roll carts to a small sale of dresses and fashion accessories. 'Where is the stage?' I asked Khuri. 'Inside.' I thought we were already inside. 'No, no! This is the outside,' said Khuri leading me through a walk way lit with mini bulbs and with paper makers indicating the seating rows according to the ticket price.

There were numerous rows of plastic chairs, steel ones and a couple of sofas designated the realms of 'small', 'big' and 'high profile' ticket buyers. Several pedestal fans were placed randomly amongst these rows to provide some relief from the heat and sweat that was building up.

We sat down a little close to one such fan in the row reserved for the hundred rupee ticket holders. 'We will get a good view of the stage from here', claimed Khuri. She was a regular here. And being a regular, she also knew a lot about its owner, Anil Thikedar. She chattered away merrily about all that she knew about him, the grand poojas he conducted and invited the whole village to, the Bihu festivities he organized....all the while I sat there unhappily wondering about my Tuesday evening that had come undone.

It was a good fifteen minutes before an announcer came onto the stage and said that the play would begin 'shortly', after a couple of local performances consisting of a dance and a song. 'The owner encourages upcoming talents', Khuri pointed out. 'He is a good man.' She said, nearly whispering into my ears, as if it was a forbidden thing to say.

The dance was indeed an entertaining one but the moment the song started, something seemed to go wrong. The singer seemed to have invited the wrath of the audience sitting in the extreme last rows, otherwise referred to as the hooligans. The singer was a young boy, no later than in his late teens and appeared to have some difficulty in holding his tune amidst all the booing.

Then, suddenly, there was a howl and a thud. A couple of persons appeared on the stage next to the boy- singer and seemed to have gotten into a fight. In no time, the shouting grew by decibels and the fighting intensified. One particularly strong fighter yelled that he could slap so hard he could make his rival see Bihu upon receiving the slap. It was meant to be a ferocious threat. His rival, equal in rowdiness, responded by shouting back that one kick from him would land his rival in Shillong. This was meant to be a violent threat.

I was amused at all this dialogue exchange.

People all around us were screaming and growing restless. 'What's happened Khuri?' I asked getting anxious that this could change into a stampede.

'Calm down, calm down. It happens', she pacified me and to drive home the point, she also pulled me towards her so that my head got buried in her heavy bosom. Uncomfortable, I freed myself moments later. By now, the police patrol unit that was stationed nearby had come into action and after having dealt with the crowd, left escorting a handful of boys.

The announcer appeared again, apologizing for this unforeseen development and hoping and requesting that for the rest of the evening, the audience would be quiet enough to enjoy the play.

All this hoopla and the day's efforts at college had worn me down and a little after the play began, I dozed off. It was only the nudges from Khuri that woke me up now and then causing me to catch a dialogue or two. So by the time the play got over, I was very glad. Kisno, in keeping with his appointment with us, dropped us home.

As I walked up the stairs, I found Mridu talking to a boy. Both of them seemed startled to see me. 'I went for a play. You should have come too, Mridu. Full of action.' I said trying to pull a filler.

'Ah, my loss! By the way, this is Arjun.' She replied.

'Oh, Hi!'

Arjun merely acknowledged the greeting with a nod. 'He had some doubts regarding today's assignments.' Mridu spoke. At eleven thirty at night? I found that a little queer but then neither was my tiredness transforming me into a conversationalist. I just managed another filler, 'Lucky you, Mridu! My students don't even bother to show up in the class, ha ha!', before inserting a hasty Good Night. A sure sign, that I needed sleep.

Leaving Mridu with her student, I came inside my own flat. After a quick change, I collapsed on the bed, my last thoughts being 'I deserved a better Tuesday evening.'

25 ME

Recognition can be a killer attribute. It can severely impair one person's options. But when you look at it from the other person's viewpoint, it can be a boon. Consider my own case for instance.

My professional affiliation to Ayote brought me instant recognition. And I did not have to work hard to achieve this. The reason behind this mindless achievement was simple. Ayote was the biggest thing happening at Imry and very few people of Imry had the opportunity to be associated with it. So the village welcomed with open arms any Ayotic to Imry, even if they were not natives of the village. This made us Ayotics interesting subjects of observation. What did we do? How did we do it? Why did we do it? When would we do it again? They had updated details on our everyday living. Such was their working knowledge of our daily routines that sometimes I felt that if I ever forget about what I had to do, I could just consult one of them.

In fact, this is what happened with respect to my to and fro-ing to the Institute. My timely arrivals and departures at the cycle rickshaw stand had become so well documented that even if I turned up at that time on an off day wanting to go someplace else, without even asking , they would first drive me to the Institute. After reaching the gates they would attain crystal clarity on my actual destination. Then, after a few anecdotes highlighting similar mishaps in a self deprecating humorous note, the rickshaw wallah would drop me where I wanted.

Provided he did not engage in any 'name calling' contest with fellow drivers on the way, to get space on the road. But more often than not, he would get entwined in at least one such fight.

'Ye thinks this ye father's rod, wat?'

'Don't ye brings mah father into dis, wat?'

'Oh yes, I brings him and his father and his father also. Huh!'

'Oh, ye wil. Wil ye?'

'Yea.'

'Wel, take dat 'n dat.'

This last dialogue invariably being the start of a series of wild gesticulations which would never get deemed as being civilized.

I never bothered with these incidents except that I found them time consuming. And then my intention would be to make peace to get on, though that seldom happened. Imryites, I found out, were broad heartedly wild and decisive. If you deserved to be sweared at, swear at you, they would, using the choicest of words. Evey rickshawallah seemed to be highly educated in them. But their lack of punctuality in ending these uncivilized exchanges bothered me. So I thought of a short cut to the dialogue process.

It would work like this:

'Ye thinks this ye father's rod, wat?'

'Wat els? Ye father in law gifted this as bride price?'

There!

To me, all further unnecessary inclusion of many more fathers should stop with this. However, the dialogue had loopholes. The most important being- it was long, roundabout and therefore difficult to keep in mind, in comparison to the set of short ones in the original version. I chucked it from proposing it to any rickshaw wallah for trial. But it was very tempting to try. Especially when after spending long hours of research and grave tracking at the library, all I wanted was to reach home as quickly as possible to sleep. Alas, I would find myself held up on the road, at the mercy of these warring folks.

I had been devoting my time at the Border War Memorial Museum, thanks to Sarat's friend who was the curator of the museum. All these social connections left me thinking that should I someday decide to write a book on Finding Mr. Bharadwaj, I would have a long list of people to acknowledge and thank.

The first time I went, I felt just like the seasoned tourist with a penchant for historical tours. I would let the curator take me through the various shelves of weapons, tools, uniforms, letters, photographs used during the wars but persistently interrupt him by blurting out whatever I had myself found out. Exactly the kind of thing a curator would be put off by and be irritated. So by the time we were done, I could see that I had annoyed him by a large degree so that the result was, I did not find out anything more or new about either of the many wars fought or about the 'Hell Pass'.

I was coldly shown the door.

But I returned soon. This time, with a much focused mind. Also, this time, I opted to keep questioning everything I saw and heard.

I asked why most of the photographs were of digging and road construction. I was curious why the surviving maps always had a bright red coloured 'X' mark at several places. I wanted to know why the supervisors shown sitting on field equipments were not always of engineer rank. I grilled the curator on how come there was so much material on war time diseases and hospital practices than anything else. I wanted a reasonable explanation on how come most of the salvaged documents from the wars were almost always about expenses in food, medicines and daily supplies.

My barrage of questions had the curator beaten.

He had hardly managed to get himself a breath after saying that the workers, who were mainly always civilians always found themselves building roads or clearing them after landslides or earthquakes, in their efforts to assist the army in marching forward to beat the enemy, when he had found himself explaining the war strategy of secret identification and destruction of the enemy's hide outs which explained the 'X' marks, again by work mostly done by civilians.

He managed a gulp of water here and barely was he done with this that, he had to get into a lengthy explanation of how even the flimsiest quarrel at the Border led to huge movement of refugees, for whom shelter, food and medication had to be arranged for. And given that in the land of 'lahe-lahe', where both time and things were slow to happen, British administration pre independence and Indian administrators post independence had learnt that they themselves had to be pretty hands-on with the ground activities that went about, if they wanted to keep the enemy at bay.

'Does that satisfy you?' Asked the curator as he felt relieved at being able to get some badly needed relaxed breathing and moped the sweat off his forehead.

'Yeah, that was indeed huge!' I thanked him.

My biggest find in this second visit was of the huge participation of civilians and the presence of refugees. Neither of these points had ever struck me. I had never considered that the missing Bharadwaj could have been a refugee or a civilian too.

After all, during the Wars, many people —natives and non natives — had moved in-out, in sizeable numbers to-from Imranpur, with both the warring armies and villagers having fallen prey to the enemy. There was heavy casualty from the war. Almost every family lost a father, son, husband or brother in the war.

'Isn't there a list of the dead?' I asked, giving voice to the wild thought that rose in my mind that they should have a record of the fallen ones, be it a soldier or a civilian. The question stumped the curator. Helping himself to yet another glass of water, he said, 'You are right. There should be. Perhaps there is. Unfortunately, I have no information on that.'

'Don't their descendants ever come to find out?' I asked irritated that my fellow brethren at Imranpur were not enthusiastic seekers of the past. 'No. People here already who they have descended from. The account runs in the family, one generation to the next. No need for records.'

Funny, that. I told myself, because this reasoning did not hold for me. I had no idea who I had descended from. And the account passed on to me by my previous generation was all warped. I looked sadly at the photographs fixed on the walls. What if Mr. Bharadwaj was one of them?

'If you want to know about someone specific, you will have to speak around to people.' The curator told me. I asked him if he had someone in his family who had been in any of these wars. 'Not mine.' He admitted. 'We moved in, in recent times. You need to talk to the old families', he said before announcing, 'Closing time'.

I left the museum with a new goal of finding out if there was another place that held more and detailed information of the War or was there someone I could talk about it.

I was returning from this exhaustive session on a Sunday evening when I had got into yet another recognition based 'passenger loading cum in-road fighting' rickshaw. It was one of those rare occasions when we did not meet another rickshaw. The trip was beginning to feel odd due to the absence of the 'swearing game' to which I had got quite used to by now. To make up for this, the rickshaw wallah struck up a conversation with me.

'Missy knws wat hapned?' He asked me.

'No, what happened?'

He delivered a rather disturbing news- Imranpur's most named and valued theatre actor had gone missing. I did not even know the village had one.

'What?' It was the only response that I could think of.

'Missy knws da aktor? No? Yes?'

'Which aktor, I mean, actor?'

'Da missin' aktor.'

'Which aktor, I mean actor, went missing?'

'Phrom ours villaze.'

It was turning out to be a redundant conversation. Theoretically, I could know any actor I wanted to and that I did. Anyone of them could have gone missing. Apparently, one of them had. Failing miserably to make any headway in the talk, I purchased a copy of the evening newspaper which had 'Rubul Kalita Goes Missing' as its headline.

Ah, what thrills in the village!

26 SAIKIA'S DAY IN THE SUN

It struck Saikia that life had suddenly turned interesting.

Very interesting. From having no cases or rather waiting for cases to happen, he now had his hands full with three cases! Of course, one of them was pretty negligible- a boy caught stage crashing at the local theatre thereby leading to assault and stampede. But the other two were substantial.

The first was the case of Rubul Kalita. The papers were abuzz about it. A section comprising largely of the actor's fans and represented in print by Dainik Imry opinioned pretty volubly. The actor had gone missing after a fall out with his boss- Anil Thikedar, they reported. It accused the Thikedar of having something definite to do with it and asked him to come clean on this. What with the current passion of high profiled people such as he, being hand in gloves with gangsters and insurgents, they would have only the truth and nothing but the truth, they demanded.

Much to the annoyance of these people, a rival group, which was represented in print by The Imranpur Times, declared Rubul Kalita as 'no great an actor to be missed for long' and that probably he had left for better shores since his sunset days were visible on the horizon of Imry. Besides, it was not correct to accuse the Thikedar, the very man who made Rubul the star he was, they declared.

As in all cases, this was sufficient for public opinion to be divided.

The Rubul-lers did not take kindly to this at all. Unable to get the upper hand through mass media dialogue, they arranged for a protest in front of the village's Administrative Office and demanded that the Officials pressurize the police to find Rubul and bring the accused to justice. The actor's son and wife visited the demonstrators, thanked them for the support and expressed hope and faith in the Officials.

In turn, the Administrators called in the police and asked them to get the crowd dispersed. Saikia led his men in cordoning off the area and spraying water on the demonstrators. Such an action was unprecedented in the history of the police force at Imranpur. But now, Saikia was changing all that.

The other case had to do with the Thikedar himself. He had called up Saikia to tell him something but he had to cut off saying he would call again.

Inspector Saikia waited excitedly.

In the meantime, he decided to sort out the simple case of that juvenile delinquent who was unbelievably ill mannered at the village theatre the previous night.

27 THE CALL

The Head of the Institute of Technical Education, Imranpur had finished the conversation and disconnected the phone. It was a weird conversation. Almost all of his work related conversations were weird but this one surpassed them all. It was civil and the language, polite. It was the content. *That* was weird. However, he was certain that he had heard it correct.

'May we come in sir?' A scared voice peeping through the door sought permission.

Under normal circumstances, he would have said, 'No, Get out'. He did not like to be disturbed by nasty fellows who would get into trouble at the drop of a chalk and then come running to him seeking forgiveness as well as protection from the Disciplinary Committee. He was capable to forgiving as well as offering the much desirable protection and he did grant them both though only on a case to case basis.

However, given the nature of the phone call that he had just attended, any distraction was welcome. He was more than willing to talk to anybody.

'Come in!'

BoNO, BoNuT and BoNTree walked in. Silence filled the air as they came face to face with the Head of the Institute.

'Yes?'

'We didn't know it was him, sir.'

'We didn't think he would take it so personally, sir.'

'We had just said something as part of the raggin- introductions, sir.'

'Okay.'

Anyway, he had come with them to watch the play, they said. He had boasted that he could do much better than the hero on the stage. This led to some three directional sledging, they agreed. Apart from that, they hadn't done anything wrong.

All of them had been sitting in the gallery. Whoever sits in the gallery, sits there due to the encouraging environ that aids such sledging behaviour. They were merely conforming to the set expectations. They had booed also. Anyway, it was he who had gone beyond expectations.

'He said he could jump onto the stage and start singing, sir.'

'We thought it was a joke, sir.'

'But it was not sir!'

'An irritating business, this', noted the Head. But then all his work related business had always been irritating. Somehow, this felt more irritating than all those.

'He' had actually got on the stage and started singing most unpretentiously. On top of that it was not even a solo one. Actually, the song was not even a duet. It was more than a duet and somewhere fell short of being a group song. Actually it consisted of two different male voices and one female voice. This excited 'him' enough to sing in three different voices.

That's where the fight started. Because, somebody sitting close to the stage started screaming at 'him'. Basically, the person was asking 'him' to get off the stage. Inspired, others joined in. It was also an opportune moment for people to take out all their unsettled or unfairly settled scores with each other, in the name of shouting at 'him'. Gradually, words had given way to action. After one point, it was neither clear who was shouting at whom nor who was beating whom. All the while Rajib Deka occupied the stage and sang his threesome song, until somebody decided enough was enough and called in the police.

'The police locked us all up, sir.'

'But because we were only booing, we were let off, sir.'

'But Rajib is still in the lock up, sir.'

'Hmm', said the Head. 'You may go now.'

'So it has finally come to this', he thought.

Rajib Deka- arrested. Nevertheless, *that* was indeed, some phone call.

28 THE ACTION PLAN

The only way to ensure that your success is better than the biggest of all successes is by poking a hole at it. So naturally, the bigger the hole, the greater the satisfaction. Right then, at Imranpur, success was personified in the form of Anil Thikedar. Poking holes at such a character ought to guarantee eternal happiness!

The only problem with this was that it could not be achieved by a one man strong army. It needed a team. And a team of this sort was what Bikash had built after much hard work.

'Dada, are you sure this is a right thing to do?' Monjit asked wiping the perspiration from his forehead with the ends of the *gamusa* hanging around his neck. He was Bikash's friend who made a living out of selling tea and fried snacks on a cart. Bikash nodded. He had faith.

Monjit though, was still finding his. He could not be blamed. Everyday morning before the start of business, he said his prayers to the framed Gods and Goddesses that he had nailed onto the roof of his cart, over half a dozen thin long incense sticks. His normal prayer requests were limited to asking them to bring in more business and to keep a watchful eye over him. So when Bikash appeared one morning just as he had finished praying and put forward this prospect to him, he did not know what sort of divine sign that was.

Mixed- was the best he could come up with. And that was why he kept asking questions to Bikash. The other team member was Biresh who worked in a garage and satisfied his urges for a high octane life by driving auto rickshaws in his spare time. Always up for a thrilling spree, he guaranteed to get the much needed vehicle.

The goals had already been identified and the plan outlined. All it now needed was getting it carried out. To make sure that they did not leave behind any trace of their activity and to prevent any kind of information leakage, they exchanged all correspondence electronically; Bikash being the brains behind this. It had taken Bikash considerable amount of pain to teach Monjit and Biresh the emailing business. But he being Bikash and the leader of his group had done it.

And there was a lot of information too. Obtained from all the surveillance that the three had carried out without attracting any undue attention to themselves except for Bikash and Biresh who carried out their side of the responsibility jointly sitting at the driver's seat of the rickshaw that Biresh was driving. This was because rickshaw drivers are the least of the chosen lot for having a civilized discourse by the majority of their passengers. And the majority of the passengers being college girls, house wives and sharp witted grannies still going strong with their razor sharp talking skills, who have since time immemorial regarded rickshaw drivers to be such uneducated dimwits of the lowest order who cheat on the fare meter, that they thought it befitting to shout at them.

This was true even if there were two of them at the driving seat which for all practical purposes seemed like two-in-one trouble. And one of them being semi educated made no difference at all.

However, despite such tarnishing to their personal brands, they did well. Especially Monjit, who had done his bit on their identified 'Gift', as he wheeled about his cart selling his tea and snacks. This turned out to be such an ingenious thing that Bikash could not help but congratulate himself on having thought of it. They now knew that their 'Gift' always ventured out around mid night for a bottle of 'that-thing-you-know'. So, *that* was the time to strike.

Finally, the day for achieving success and respect had arrived. They had successfully conducted a dry run the day before to get a near feel of the actual thing. 'Say what, are we ready?' Bikash asked his buddies. They nodded in the affirmative.

At 11:30 p.m, a red TATA Magic glided noiselessly through the central road of the village, coming to a halt near the Maharani Theaters at the Market Crossroads. Parking it casually to a side, the driver got out. He shuffled about for a minute or so before pulling out a bidi and lighting it, began to smoke. When he was done, he pulled out a bottle of cheap country liquor and began emptying it.

'Bikash da', a whisper came from within the Magic. It was Monjit. Left with Biresh alone inside the vehicle, he was feeling insecure and scared. 'Come in, please', he requested.

Disgruntled but having sufficiently refreshed himself, he got back into the Magic. But not before he made sure that there weren't any bidi butts or liquor cap or bottle carelessly strewn about. He had read sufficient crime fictions to train his brain to look out for these 'clues' that could give them away.

At 11:40 p.m, a figure ventured out of the Theaters and moved steadily ahead.

At 11:45 p.m, it passed by the waiting Magic.

Two minutes later, a group of bodies got out of the magic and started shadowing the shadow of the figure. One minute later, a white handkerchief was pushed under the nose of the shadow from behind.

'Gifted!' Whispered one of the bodies. Thirty seconds later, the shadow was captured by the Magic-ians.

'Return gifted!'
'Aye, good man, done!'

Wrapping up the shadow in layers of thick blankets, everybody returned to the vehicle and making sure there wasn't another soul around, left the scene.

29 SAIKIA'S SECOND CALL

Inspector Saikia finally received his much anticipated call.

'I have called you to say that my new lead actor has been kidnapped and the kidnappers have been calling me to talk ransom.' Saikia felt his heart jump to his mouth. So this was it- that Rubul had got kidnapped and now there was ransom being asked. He shivered with excitement. This matter had to be sorted with a lot of discipline and intelligence, he decided. Saikia pulled himself together and got into action.

'You will have to come here and file an FIR for that.'

'I know.'

'So why aren't you doing it?'

Really, some people could be so silly, he thought.

'Because I thought I should give you a heads up.'

'I will regard that FIR as the heads up.'

'It involves a boy. So I thought you might have some sensitivity to take care of.'

Saikia felt an annoying tinge in his ear when he heard the Thikedar say 'boy'. Rubul Kalita was no boy. He gave a sarcastic laugh before reminding the Thikedar that his lead actor was a middle aged, married man with a grown up son who was long past his boyhood days. 'So, sir, I don't know what sensitivities you are talking about here', he said.

'You think it's Rubul I am talking about?'

'Of course! Are you not?'

'Why would I? Rubul isn't my man anymore!' The Thikedar reminded the inspector of Rubul's unceremonious departure once again. Saikia was puzzled.

The Thikedar made it very clear from the beginning of the conversation itself that Rubul had left his employment of his own free will before he had gone missing. So, he had nothing to do with it.

'Hah! Didn't they always say that?' The inspector told himself. Further, to his trained mind, this qualified the Thikedar to be the last man to have seen Rubul. 'My number one man for interrogation', he noted.

'If it isn't Rubul, then who is kidnapped?'

'Didn't I tell you that it is my new lead actor who has been kidnapped?'

'And who is that? Doesn't he have a name?'

'Rajib Deka of Institute of Technical Education.'

Saikia froze.

'What???' He asked when he felt he had recovered a little. This call was becoming way too exclamatory in nature.

'Are you sure?'

'What do you mean?'

'I mean are you sure it is Rajib Deka of Institute of Technical Education?'

'What makes you think I am making it up?'

'He.. he.. well, he.. he..'

'What's funny? Is that funny? Don't think that's funny.'

'No.. he..he..'

'That wasn't a joke. What's wrong with you Inspector?'

'No..joke…he..he..', Saikia wanted to explain something about Rajib Deka but decided against it.

'You didn't inform the Institute?' He asked instead.

'What makes you think I didn't? The Head of the Institute had a tough time accepting it though. Said it was the weirdest thing he had ever heard.'

'Oh, well, okay. You file FIR for Rajib Deka.'

'Of course, Inspector. But know this, I have nothing to do with that Rubul bugger and two, find my boy-Rajib.'

'err… Couldn't he have just gotten back to college?'

'I heard the kidnappers threaten and Rajib's muffled cries over phone. You think this is funny?'

'What? No..No way… Not anymore.'

'They bloody had the guts to send me an email telling me this!'

'What???' Saikia was finding it increasingly difficult to believe his ears. Never had criminals been this tech savvy in Imranpur.

But right then, what intrigued him was that the case involved Rajib Deka. Possibly there was more than one Rajib Deka, thought Saikia. He would have to check with the institute again. He assured the Thikedar on the matter and the Thikedar arranged to have his men go to file the case. 'An email, damn it!' Saikia heard the Thikedar thunder as he hung up.

Saikia lay back on his chair getting rather entangled in his thoughts. However neatly he tried to organize the facts, he kept getting tangled at two points. One, where is Rubul Kalita if he has not been kidnapped. Two, how come Rajib Deka got *kidnapped?*

Surely, something was wrong.

Because, he had Rajib Deka in his lock up all through the night and in the morning, had called the Principal of the Technical Institute to come and get his ward. Could it be that on way to the college he got kidnapped? Well, in that case it should have been the Principal calling him up. Not Anil Thikedar. The more Saikia thought about what connected Rajib and the Thikedar, the more he felt convinced of his first theory that there were two Rajib Dekas in the Institute. He would have to speak to the Head on this.

'Damn complicated business, this.' Saikia muttered to himself as he set to work.

'Excuse me, sir?'

A look of being haunted came over Saikia's face. It took him all the courage he could gather to turn around to see who was speaking. It was I. Seeing me, he was certainly relieved but I could see in his eyes the doubt of whether I was an apparition.

'Yes?'

'Could I speak to Inspector Saikia?'

'I am Saikia.'

'Oh good, I am Ashima Brendon from Institute of ….'

Saikia froze a second time and I am quite sure I heard him mutter 'uh, no not again'. 'I need your help', I continued.

After what the curator at the Museum had told me I had decided that in a place like Imry, if there was one person I could ask about war, it had to be someone who had something to do with law and order and again, given that I was seeking such information in a place like Imry, the best person was, I realized, Inspector Saikia.

'What help?' I noted continued suspicion in his tone.

'Would you know anyone here who has had a relative who was part any War?'

I must have definitely uttered some magic word, for I saw the expressions on the Inspector's face change instantly to show pride and honour and when he told me that he himself hailed from an illustrious family whose sons had been to wars, I knew I had done the right thing.

'In fact, my grandfather has fought Wars!'

'Oh! Then I would like to speak to him.'

'Sure.'

'Err… how and where do I meet him?' Somehow there was an assumption that I knew the grandfather. It was the Imry standard. It never occurred to them that you could *not* know someone if you lived in Imry. You knew everyone and everyone knew you. That was almost some kind of law onto itself.

'Wait… one of my constables will take you there.' He called for one of his men and by the time the fellow showed up, Saikia scribbled out a note. 'Give this to him. It's sort of a reference from me. He will feel freer talking, so.'

I took the note and thanking him left the Station accompanied by the constable. I did not turn around to see him as I walked away, but I had a feeling that Saikia rubbed his hands in glee. I am not sure if it was because I had made his day but I knew that I had definitely taken a step closer to finding the uncertain Mr. Bharadwaj.

30 A TEACHER'S SUSPICION

Dr. Hiramoni Nath, Ph.D was, for all academic purposes, a woman of scientific temperament. From the way she sat on her chair- a picture of 'A Scientist Engrossed in Thoughts'- to the way she demonstrated the various experiments in lab-'A Scientist On The Verge of Discovering The Next Big Thing', whatever the next thing was. It was something she had achieved with resounding success on the campus of University of Melbourne.

She didn't take anything at face value. Rather, she couldn't. She was used to thinking, reasoning, listening, asking questions, debating and most important of all, staying open minded when all else failed to give her the very answers which she sought.

Characteristics, which were precisely responsible for the astute observation she had made about one of her newly joined colleague in the Department of Computer Science & Engineering. Which was this- *there is something wrong with her.*

But for the moment, this was only a hypothesis and she would have to work real hard to prove it. She considered the known, well established facts first.

She, her colleague that is, was a well educated, successful woman having worked in India's top IT company for five years and now had joined the Institute of Technical Education, Imranpur.

Nothing unusual about that. It happens. She was engaged to an equally if not more, well educated, successful man. Nothing unusual about that. It happens.

So, then…

Here, Dr. Hiramoni's brain had to take a sort of u-turn in its thinking. And given that the next set of facts to be considered were not easy, her face winced in pain. That's where her scientific training came to her rescue- she was able to get past it and continue her thinking.

So, then…

Why was she seen last Sunday at The Guwahati City Multiplex with someone who was not even a quarter as educated as her, let alone be successful?

The person in question was a final year male student at the Institute of Technical Education, Imranpur who had been in the final year for the past three years. Why was she walking around with someone who was not her fiancé at eleven o' clock in the night at a public place?

The person in question was last known from reliable sources, which included the Head of the Institute, a recovering alcoholic. He had been thrown out from the esteemed Assam State Engineering College, for having been in no condition to pay any attention to his studies precisely due to this very habit.

Therefore, Dr Hiramoni Nath seemed to be coming to some kind of a conclusion. She would prefer not to be disturbed by anything or anyone at this crucial moment. She was getting there…yes, she knew it… therefore, this new colleague,…that woman, she was…she was…she…

'Hullo Hiramoni baidou!' The maths teacher announced her grand arrival at the staff room, at that moment. Dr. Madhobi Talukdar, Ph.D had a different approach to things and in general to life when compared with Dr. Hiramoni, despite what her credentials seemed to convey about her.

Her modus operandi, if it could be called that, in the kind of situations that Dr. Hiramoni was in, would be something quite upfront and totally unapologetic. A fact Dr. Hiramoni found very difficult to approve of and she believed the reasons for this was that Dr Madhobi's Ph.D was an Indian one. As per her, an Indian Ph.D was not 'competent enough'.

'Hello baidou!' She repeated herself having got no response to her earlier salutation. 'Huh? oh, Hi!' Dr. Hiramoni replied a little absent mindedly at first and then realizing that having done so had cut her off from arriving at the slippery truth which she was investigating, became angry.

'What happened? Why are you looking annoyed, baidou?' Dr. Madhobi enquired.

'I was nearly there-'

'Where?'

'Getting the answer.'

'Of what, baidou?'

'Of what this Mridu is up to.'

'What is this Mridu upto, baidou?' Dr. Madhobi's eyes began to gleam in delight. Surely, this Mridu had some skeletons in her cupboard. Why else would Baidou say this, she told herself.

'Silly woman', Dr. Hiramoni thought to herself. 'Wasn't that what I was trying to find out?' Aloud, she said, 'That is exactly the thing, Madhobi'. 'That is what I am trying to find out'. This was a proof of superiority of the foreign Ph.D over its Indian counterpart.

'But how can you find that out sitting here, baidou?'

What was this woman trying to say?

'You must be going and talking to her, finding out from people, thinking will not help!'

'Why will she tell me such things, Madhobi?'

'Well, then you must find alternate means of finding out.'

'Like?'

'Like…like…' Dr. Madhobi found herself a little tight in offering suggestions, when suddenly an idea flashed through her brain. 'Keep an eye on her', she said.

'You mean spy?'

'Well..no.. I guess..well..'

Pretending to do one thing while intending another was what Madhobi had in her mind, she clarified. 'And how exactly will that work?'

'I have an idea', said the Indian PhD holder, for once superseding the credibility of the one from Melbourne- with the secret interest of enabling to topple hidden skeletons in secret cupboards, of course.

31 SISTA CODE

Being susceptible to powerful ideas can be quite contagious. At least that is what Dr. Hiramoni had found out, once she heard of the idea that the maths teacher had told her. Though initially, she had shook her head and said a firm 'no'. But Madhobi had been insistent. 'Listen no, baidou', she kept on. 'What is the harm?'

It wasn't the harm factor that had bothered Hiramoni. She, too, realized that there was no harm. For her, it had more to do with her beliefs. She didn't believe in the kind of stuff her younger colleague did. And she didn't believe in them because such things like 'spying' and 'pretending' had not found their way into her value system that was dominated by 'free-will', 'freedom' etc. So understandably, she had found it difficult to make it a part of her.

However, the more Madhobi kept talking about it, the more the idea infiltrated Hiramoni's mind. It delayed her sleep at night, woke her up in the middle of the night, made her rise in the morning before the alarm could; stayed with her all through her morning schedule for the family; circled her head in the silent moments in the class while her students were solving numericals; chanted in her ears while she ate her lunch with the other teachers and stared at her as she did her course work correction, prompting even her husband to ask her, 'What's up Hira?'

That is when she realized that, this idea must be powerful. Otherwise why would she feel haunted by it? Yes, this idea was *indeed* powerful.

She *must* act on it. Madhobi gave her a triumphant smile when she told her that this idea had her green light. 'Come, now no time to be lost', said Madhobi. Having being the brains behind the plan, Madhobi now set to script out every action to be enacted as a part of it. She even took to playing the role of director and reviewer, which reduced Hiramoni to being a puppet which strangely, didn't seem to bother her.

In accordance with the plan, she spent a couple of days in developing 'friendship' with Mridu by showing up at the water cooler at the same time as she did, happily exclaiming, 'What coincidence!' Then she proceeded to tell Mridu that there was this 'horrible' program of chemical equations which she needed to run and understand but just could not. So could she ask Mridu for help? Mridu having unsuspectingly agreed to this, Hiramoni told her she would give it to her at the earliest since it was urgent.

Here, Madhobi's script needed Hiramoni to act forgetfulness on this matter, something Hiramoni was not good at since she had a special ability to remember every detail with high precision even if it had happened a decade ago. However, barring some minor glitches, this was taken care of and as per the plan, Hiramoni showed up at Mridu's quarter at ten in the night with the 'horrible' program in question.

'Must be my age, no? Always forgetting!' She attempted small talk as Mridu opened the door but did not let her in. 'Ok, ma'am. I will have a look at this and get back to you.' She said and was about to say Good Night and shut the door, when Hiramoni remembered that the purpose of this visit was to get inside Mridu's house 'to look for signs'. 'But my dear, I have to explain it, else how will you know where I am getting stuck?' So saying she made her way past a worried Mridu and went inside. Mridu tried to block her way saying, she would ask her the next day and almost succeeded in this when from inside Arjun's voice called out, 'Mridu!'

Pretending not to have recognized the owner of the voice, Hiramoni said 'oh, sorry,… so sorry, sorry' and then took her leave. The next day she reported this to Madhobi who brimmed with satisfaction. It also occurred to Hiramoni that as part of the idea, only she seemed to be the doer and that too, a lot of it. As per the original plan, Madhobi also had a crucial part to play. 'I have, baidou!' She confirmed, her eyes twinkling. Three years at the Institute had not only made her familiar with the staff but it had also given her an insider's status on who was related to whom, how and why. And for the purpose of this plan, she had tapped into this knowledge.

A 'chance' conversation with the college bus driver on the purchase of coconut laddoos revealed that he had an aunt who lived next to the staff campus and took contracts to prepare and deliver coconut laddoos. This was enough for Madhobi to 'meet' this aunt while out on her evening walk and become friendly with her. Eventually, an invitation to tea was extended and general chit-chat ensued that revolved around life, family, society, college, students, colleagues...

It was during the course of this that the woman was able to speak out what had been 'troubling' her mind for the past good many days. Now, finding an outlet in the most compassionate spirit of Dr. Madhobi Talukdar, she confessed that her heart was full of pity and grief because 'that poor girl Mridu is pining for her fiancé'. The maid servant who also worked for her had said this.

Yes, yes, there have been many tasteless fights- lot of swearing, shouting and crying- over phone. And now, there is a new boyfriend. There have been very late night going-ons, coming-outs and carrying-ons. Yes, yes, the maid would confirm it. In fact, she did confirm it.

'I hear this new boy is actually a student in the college?', the woman asked. Madhobi pretended not to know. 'Is it?' She asked, pretending to be surprised at this disclosure. 'Could be. It is such a huge college, baidou! How can I know? Anyway, it is her life, no? If educated and decent people like you and me start poking our nose into others business, what will people say?'

With that, both the women continued with their tea and discussion on coconut laddoos, all the while knowing perfectly well that the new resident at Flat Number 102, B Block was indeed a student of the Institute of Technical Education, Imranpur by the name- Arjun.

32 SAIKIA'S GRANDFATHER

Saikia had told me during my short conversation with him at the Police Station that day, that his grandfather was a 'river of information on war'. 'It's almost as if he has always lived his life through one war onto the other', he had said. My mind knew only one river and it was this that caused it to register in my mind, a certain kind of image of Saikia's grandfather- a figure mighty and majestic, at once. What greeted me however was a tall, thin man of delicate frame supported on a walking stick with a head full of hair and a shine in his eyes.

Sitting on a rocking chair with his feet up on a *murha*, he greeted me. 'You must be the girl Babu was telling me about'. Babu, I figured was what Saikia was called at home.

'Yes, koka.' I replied as I conveyed the traditional folded hands gesture of respect to him. He seemed ancient. I did not know what to expect of him- senile decay, disillusionment or a general sense of resignation to life. I would have to wait to have some conversation with him to find out more on that.

Kokadeuta, Assamese for grandfather, regarded me with

curiosity. I could sense that from his glances. Guess it wasn't everyday someone from my generation took an interest to meeting and discussing war with him. 'Sit down, *ma-joni*', he said, pointing to a chair near to where he was sitting. *Ma-joni*- little girl- that was definitely me, given that koka was so old.

'Assistant professor at that institute, is it?' 'Yes, koka', I blushed a little. Assistant Professor was a weighty title for me. Nowhere near an average conversationalist, I feared that the small talk would soon die out leaving nothing more to discuss about. However, I managed the customary, how are you.

'Oh, never mind me. I am still quite a bunch!' He chuckled. 'How are *you*? You look all disoriented by the walking to reach here.' That certainly was true.

The many lanes and by-lanes that criss-crossed Imranpur, made residence tracing a game of crossing the maze. It was a good thing that Saikia had sent along the constable, for it would have been difficult for me to locate the house where his grandfather stayed. Once there, I thanked the constable and sent him off only to wonder a little later how would I return. Deciding that probably the return was deemed to be an adventure, I went ahead to meet the man himself.

Koka proposed tea.

'You drink tea, *ma-joni*?'

'Yes, koka.'

'Good, then let's ask the boy to get us tea.'

I thought I would have to go calling for this boy but Koka got up and walking to the door, gave out a call, 'Oi luara, aiphale ah. Sah bona!' It was a specific 'Hey Boy, come here and make tea' shout to convey the message. Having spared of this work, I instead got up and paced around the room. I stopped at the tall table in the room. There was an old bag on the top of it. It looked like those bags that army men have with them. I looked at it curiously. 'Bring that bag here, *ma-joni*'.

Koka said as he returned to his chair. I came back with the bag. After sitting down, he extracted the contents of the bag. They were papers and koka seemed to be engrossed in some searching activity.

'Need help, koka?' I offered. 'Oh, no, no.' He refused. 'Even if it is needed I will not ask, you see. These are my most precious papers!' So saying he grinned. 'War papers?' I did not want to sound intrusive but the temptation to ask had got the better of me. 'Yes!' Koka's sunken eyes brightened up.

'Saikia writes that you want to know about wars'. So, that was what Saikia had been scribbling in the paper. 'I just wanted to talk to you about them.' I was not sure if I wanted to read and see the old man's papers. Besides, that would be time consuming and somehow I was not feeling patient over the matter.

'You want to ask something?'

'Hmm.'

We were interrupted by the delivery of tea and sweets here. The boy laid out a small table with two cups of tea, a plate of snacks and a spare saucer. I waited for koka to begin his tea. I found him emptying half his cup of tea into the empty saucer. 'That's for Aditi.'

'A granddaughter. Possibly Saikia's daughter.' I thought to myself. Koka gave a low, long whistle. It was certainly a unique way for summoning a granddaughter but I should have guessed better. A couple of minutes later, I heard mewing at the door and lo, a cat pranced into the room with its tail up in the air.

'Meet Aditi, *ma-joni*', said koka. I had never met cats in person like this or on any earlier social occasion. Certainly, it felt quite a novel thing to do. I said 'Hi' and scratched its head and, like all cats that I have met before, I was welcomed by a cold paw. 'She drinks tea?' A cat that relishes tea was new to me, too. 'My Aditi loves to drink tea'.

I admitted to Koka that Aditi was a most unusual cat. 'She is', he confirmed.

'You know,' began Koka, after the first sip of his cup. 'War is all that I know.' He said, looking first at me and then fixing his gaze onto the horizon. I half suspected that he saw various scenes from his many war lives flash past his eyes.

'Were you born in one?'

My question seemed to have brought him out of the trance. Though the question startled him, he looked at me and smiled one of his toothless smiles before replying, 'Very strangely no.' He had been born in the relatively quieter times. 'But let me tell you this, I celebrated my entry into teenage with the Quit India movement!' He said triumphantly, his little eyes twinkling and widening into the still bushy eyebrows above them.

'Oh wow!' I exclaimed before making the suggestion that this was a most noble and patriotic act requiring a lot of courage while being exceptionally dangerous as well. Probably it had caused him to be regarded as some kind of a teen hero. He gave me one of those looks that teachers give to the students who have not read their lessons correctly. 'Nothing of the sort.'

This was, I inferred, a mild rebuke because, as he went on to tell later, doing everything to get the British to Quit India seemed to be the only thing to do when he had turned a teen. Everybody was doing it.

Nevertheless, Koka had his moment of fame when he happened to be standing next to a boy of his age who had taken the direct blow of a policeman's *lathi* during a march taken out by the student's union against the foreign rulers. This boy happened to be the son of a lawyer who himself was in jail for having offered 'satyagraha'. Needless to say, the matter became big and then turned ugly when the boy succumbed to his injuries.

'It was horror and terror after that', reported Koka. A most expected reaction, I agreed remembering from my history books that, that was a time when the nation as a whole was gnawing at the British pretty ruthlessly. 'My father thrashed me and packed me off to a distant relative to be tutored at home.'

'Oh!'

'I was there until independence came about.'

Koka was exiled from an atmosphere that was charged with patriotic fervor. Not since the time of Maniram Dewan, had people been this electrified by their passion for a movement. If it was the British tea planters at the time of the Dewan; now it was the British Administration. Strictly speaking, not much of a difference, but still.

If '*Maniram Dewan bor bhal manuh asil O!*' (Maniram Dewan was a very good man) that was sung then, out of grief at his execution, now it was a time for songs like 'Boys on this side of the Brahmaputra shall die fighting till their last breath' by the illustrious poet Aggarwala and the poetic implores to the Brahmaputra to make its people as mighty as itself for the fight, from the Bard of the land. The vigor of the new resurgent attitude expressed in these latest songs showed how much Koka had missed out. However, Saikia super senior differed in his ideology when it came to the discharge of patriotic duties. Or maybe he was learning from the mistakes committed by the various patriarchs in the Saikia ancestry.

For instance, somewhere around in the late 1880s, the earliest known Saikia patriarch had got deeply inspired by a club for Assamese literature development that was founded in Calcutta. It was fired by fierce Assamese nationalist sentiments. These sentiments made an impression on him and accordingly, he had set up a local chapter of this in his village.

In a matter of a decade, this club got transformed into a students' union. By then, this patriarch had moved on from life but his devotion towards the union had been ingrained in his son. This new patriarch saw the union turn into a student literary association in the mid of the next decade. His untimely demise spared him from being witness to what happened next.

Now, it was Saikia super senior's turn to assume the role of the patriarch and with it, inherit the love for the literary association. In his life time, he saw the association split into two, one calling itself a Student Federation and the other becoming a Student Congress.

But when over the course of ten years, the two units failed to make any significant impact on the people, they agreed to merge and go back to being a Students' Union. So, in all probability, Saikia super senior had seen the futility of it all and was determined not to let the same fate befall his son. And he began by keeping the family's relation with the Union, a secret from him while side by side, he distanced himself from it so much so that by the time of 'Quit India', he was a discarded member of it.

Now that Saikia super senior had learnt from history, he had decided that instead of giving in to the signs of the times, he would be more future focused. Since independence was due anyway, he felt that it was only right to be educated enough so as to be ready to make good use of it when it finally came through.

I could now understand the 'horror and terror' that the then teenaged koka had to go through on having to stay away from the heat of this excitement. I supposed that it was this suppressed desire that must have made him to participate in all of the subsequent wars.

'Not at all.' He declared. He had in fact, got himself a neat little job at one of those tea estates. A few years later, the State found itself at war with a neighbor from the north, China. This was the beginning of the list of wars that koka was going to find himself in. A few years thereafter; he saw action in another war, this time supporting a neighbour on the south for their independence.

In time to come though, the warring neighbours stopped being international. Instead, the fights were now across the state borders. Having been drafted into the army, he ended up battling each one of them.

It was always the same case of overstepping the borders. Be it a change of season, the government or time, it was the State boundary that always suffered and the people living around it who bore the brunt of it. Then there were the maps, circulated in secrecy, without constitutional authority about it. As for sending armed forces or negotiations, these things never seemed to matter. It was only in the last two decades that the intensity of these matters had come down. Sporadic incidents still sparked sufficient tension but not to the level that had led to a repeat of the violence that had occurred in the June of 1985 at Merapani.

I had finished my tea by now. But Koka had not. I offered to warm it up for him. He dismissed the idea, instead pouring the remains in his cup onto Aditi's saucer. The cat gleefully lapped it up.

Armed with a photo of his taken in army uniform, he began to tell his story of how as a young man he worked at the tea estate but with the commencement of war, came about to be enrolled in the army.

'Chinese aggression', he said. That is how the war with China had remained in public memory. The army was losing, retreating. People were fleeing their homes. Koka, along with the surviving men from his unit were on the run when they came under intense firing and shelling. Trying to save himself from the splinters, Koka had bumped into a rock that knocked him unconscious and rolled him away, separating him from the others.

He gained consciousness at the edge of a deserted village. He was surprised at being alive, amidst dead cattle and burnt houses. Keeping to the destruction for cover, he crawled his way to the nearest camp where he learnt that most of his companions had been killed and a couple of the remaining taken as prisoners.

'My childhood friend was one of them', he said as his wrinkled hands straightened out an old newspaper cutting and held it out for me to see.

'Sylhet was easier.' He continued, his voice sounding relaxed.

Of course. There was no humiliation to be experienced in assisting the Mukti Bahini in achieving its freedom. But having been posted to the Communication Corps for this assignment, Koka saw no live action.

'One must be careful in choosing profession. You risk inspiring others'.

'What is wrong with that koka?'

'My sons got inspired to join the army.'

Though it was not koka who was the inspirer. That credit went to the legend of the soldier at the Jaswant Garh, who died defending his post against the Chinese and whose ghost still patrolled the area. In fact, he still got his promotion, salary and leave. Stories of his war time heroics reached the ears of the children. Saikia's father and uncle were among them. And the next thing Koka knew when on home leave was that, his sons were in the army.

With father and sons, all in the army, the family attained iconic status in the village. But destiny had a cruel twist in store. The unlikely battlefield of Merapani claimed his elder son's life, when fighting alongside the Assam Police against those of Nagaland over a wretched dispute over the border.

Bhupen was this son's son who now ran Imry's only touring agency and a Magic service. Saikia's father continued with the on field activities. But his career was cut short when he contracted a bad case of malaria and never really recovered from it to be fit enough for active service. He was later posted as the Head at the local Army dispensary.

'Your job must have been pretty exciting', I said. 'At times yes, at times no', said Koka. 'You wanted to ask something?' He asked for the second time that evening. 'Kind of', I replied, feeling a little ashamed and afraid of coming across as an information encroacher. We were discussing wars that had built a personal connect with a lot of families, simply by involving them in it, in various capacities and I did not want to rub into old wounds with my quest.

'Did your father serve in any war?'

'Yes.'

'Which one?'

'I don't know.'

I told him what I learnt from the letter, not giving out much into my two father shadowed life. 'Bharadwaj, did you say?'

'Yes.'

This was followed by a long, much anticipated pause.

'I know one but he had died in a plane crash.'

'There were more?' I was surprised.

'That is what I remember. The papers were full of one Bharadwaj one day and another the next day.'

I had never considered that there could be multiple Bharadwajs to identify from. All along my thoughts had been that it was a straightforward case of finding the right person who may have met him. But now, I realized that this was now going to be very difficult for me as I had no other clue about him except for his name. From wondering how I was going to find out who he actually was, I was now disturbed by the new question of which one was he really.

'You have never seen him?'

'No.'

'Damn those wars!' Said koka, his grip on his walking stick tightening. It was almost as if he had thumped it onto the ground to make his point. Once again he appeared lost. Wars and battles have a habit of leaving behind trails of broken homes and losses of every kind. Sometimes they create by-products too, who get caught in these cross fires. Ones like me.

'I could not be with her as she lay dying.' The words came almost as a whisper. Did I also notice a tear? Perhaps. I placed a hand over koka's, the one with which he was still holding his stick. Patting his hand in silence, I felt a tear drop land on the back of my hand and escape onto the ground.

This is what the war had left us with.

33 NEWSPAPERS IN ACTION

Newspapers in Imry rarely had any raving news. Now and then, they did have the spicy story to report like the time when Saikia suffered the bombs thrice in a row, the disappearance of Rubul Kalita and the latest episode of Rajib Deka getting deposited in the police lock up; but for a major part of the time, they only had mundane things to report of. During those times, they would fill up their news spaces with tit-bits from various online gossip sites causing confusion in the minds of newcomers to Imry who found the demographics mismatching with the news content.

Consider this- a rickshawallah being fed the top ten fashion choices of the latest American reality show celebrity after her split from that hulk she had been seen roaming around with. Ta-da!

These were times when it made one wonder why did the papers even exist. But somehow that in itself seemed to provide me with some kind of a motivation. A motivation to provide the papers with some useful, constructive news. I figured that if I told my story to the papers and got them to publish it, maybe, it would reach somebody in some corner of Imry who could hand me the answers to the questions I was searching for.

Of course I was talking to Saikia's koka on this. But what if there were other families too, who were doing a similar search? I could most certainly connect and speed up matters.

Fuelled by this thought, it was not long before I found myself, first in the offices of The Imranpur Times and later in the rooms of Dainik Imry. My hunch was right. They were, indeed, fascinated. After all, it was not always that they came across a person in search of a father lost in war, decades after the war was done and over with.

But the enthusiasm that they showed for listening to the story certainly did not translate to sincerity in putting it to words for the paper. The Imranpur Times put it as a 'Citizen's Story' on their weekend supplement while the Dainik Imry put it as an article which read more like an advert on search for a missing family member.

Certainly I was disappointed but then I reminded myself that I was telling journalists a story that, for all practical purposes appealed only to me. I had cut out the 'two dad dilemma' and just focused on the 'unknown father' angle who went by the name of 'Bharadwaj' and in the process ended up insisting that they use just my first name. I had to be grateful that they had indeed considered giving the story some print space. However, from the way it was put up, I had given up all hopes of having that cold trail set ablaze, again.

I was wrong.

A couple of days after this, I got a call from the journalist of The Imranpur Times, that someone would like to meet me- a tea planter by the name Dinesh Barua. My heart beat faster. Was I finally about to get it all going again? I asked the journalist to convey that I would like to meet Dinesh Barua.

34 OUR NEIGHBOUR AT WAR

Dinesh Barua was already at the Dunlop Hill when I had arrived shielding myself under an umbrella against the unseasonal rain and trying to not get into the mud as I climbed the steps to the restaurant. He appeared to be a man of average built and height. His crisp blue shirt under the blazer tucked into a pair of black trousers, well polished leather shoes and gold rimmed spectacles resting on his dimpled face confirmed that he was above the average in society.

To stand out this prim and proper despite the rains, either he had been waiting for a long time or he moved around with staff that brushed and pressed him up every now and then. That too, would be an above the average sort of thing to do. And when he rose from his seat as I greeted him and shook hands, I knew that this was a man who had in all probability received his education abroad and knew his business. Well, he was after all a tea planter. It was his business to know his business.

We ordered tea and sandwiches and then got talking.

'So, the wars interest you', he noted. I thought that was obvious from the news report I had put out. But I guessed that he was doing more of a context setting for the things yet to be discussed. 'Well, they do seem to hold the key to my search.' I said.

He looked at me with raised eyes, his gaze coming to be fixed on me. Leaning back in his chair, he let out a deep breath and nodded his head. 'Very well', he said. It gave way to a couple of minutes of silence during which our tea was served and more people streamed in. Pouring a little milk and sugar into his tea cup and stirring it, he enquired how much I knew. How much? Oh, I could laugh at that one.

I had never bothered with history. At least not until 'the letter' had arrived. I admitted that I was not a history buff, in case he was expecting my response along those lines. I only knew what I could gather from my online reading. Most of the wars fought here had to do with changing/ annexing some disputed territory with 'the neighbours', of whom there were many.

As for Merapani, I only knew what I had heard from Koka. First the police and then the army exchanged fires and killed many. But all that it brought was only temporary peace. Loot, plunder and destruction was the reality which was kept in check with the guns. It did not have a start date and going by the current state of affairs, had not ended either. Nor was it likely to.

'But it was worse back then in the eighties', said Mr. Barua. 'The worst.' I noticed the emphasis on the 'worst' that was spoken with a tinge of disapproval. I admitted that I wouldn't know the specifics.

'People blame history for all this violence.'

'It is *not*?'

'The problem is not because of history. The problem is that there are people taking wrong advantage of history.' Mr. Barua told me. 'The past exists for a reason. The present can of course change it. But there is a way to it.'

'Meaning?'

'It is simple', he began.

Settling the border issue is more like reversing decisions taken centuries ago by a foreign power. So it had to be sorted out through talks between the governments. But there were groups-still are-against this. While they spoke of universal brotherhood, they were backed by militant outfits and so, in parallel, worked underground to break the spirit of their own words. They were loose groups, scattered everywhere, living a double faced life- running their own business while all the time living out of money paid for carrying out violence.

While they had a free hand to carry out all of their operations, the directive had always been clear – to never be caught alive. But, who gave the directions, has remained a question.

'We never knew who the original mastermind was.' He said.

'We know now?' I asked.

'Yes. But then we also know everything else about them, including that they are directionless now.'

'So that doesn't make us fear them anymore?' I concluded. Mr. Barua nodded in agreement. No wonder then that we are overpowering them always of late, I noted.

But in the eighties, it was different. The unknown mastermind and the lack of not knowing its whereabouts was a real terror. They first struck at the tea garden. It was on 'their' land, they claimed.

At first, it was the assault on the workers in the garden. Then, digging up random sections of the garden. In the second wave of attack, they resorted to looting and kidnapping- first, the employees and then, the estate owners. Finally came the ferocious round of attacks where the goal was assassination.

'My father was on the hit list', said Mr. Barua. Dinesh's father, Hiten Barua, the richest tea planter in the country did not fear being attacked. He liked being prepared to fend off the attacks. But for that, he realized, the police would not suffice. He appointed his own set of personal guards whom he got trained at his own expenses.

'One of his guards was a man named Bharadwaj.'

I now sat up feeling more interested. I wanted him to continue. 'Was there any attack at all on your father?' I asked. A prompt reply came in the positive. I was a little scared to ask what happened next. 'It was a deadly attack.'

While Hiten Barua's band of four guards managed to shield their boss from the attack, they themselves fell to it- three of them, on the spot while the fourth, Bharadwaj, managed to retain some breath on him although very feeble.

'Any idea what became of him?'

'In all likelihood he too must have died. I only remember the chaos in which my father was brought in after being attacked.'

'And what became of him, your father?'

'He made it through.'

A hush followed this.

'This is what that Bharadwaj looked like', he said producing a photo from the pocket of his blazer. It wasn't much to look at having faded. But I could make out a pair of piercing eyes and a light moustache. Otherwise he seemed quite fairly featured. This seemed like the finale for the evening. For thereafter, Mr. Barua paid the bill and we left Dunlop Hill.

35 THE TRUTH

The Head of the Institute of Technical Institute, Imranpur never failed to live up to his reputation of being a strategic personality. Though very few people actually knew what that meant, almost everyone had experienced it at least once. So, the Ayotic public knew what to expect of him, at all times.

It had to do with his preparedness. He liked to have all information at his disposal before he could strategize. The Ayotic public recognized this as a true sign of intelligence because it was so distinguishably distinct from certain other people. People like Minal Borthakur who managed the hostels, for instance. People like her decided first and then went about trying to find reasons why the decision taken made sense. This caused a lot of inconvenience to a lot of people because most of the time this led to unnecessary movement of hostellers and furniture between rooms. She would always claim that it was in the 'best interest of the hostellers'. That seldom happened. Antony Asoke Baruah could testify that. He had as many as five roommates in six months but in whose 'best interests', he hadn't been able to figure out.

Now, the Head of the Institute was not such a person. Of course, he too took decisions keeping in mind the 'best interests'. But he had a proper style of going about it. He had demonstrated that many times in the past. Like during the admission process. He was one of those few people who gathered all information about the applicant and having them spread out before him during the interview, decided to accept or reject the prospective student. He took informed decisions and THAT was not an easy thing to do, for the information could be misleading at times. Consider, for instance, Rajib Deka's score card.

When Rajib had arrived for the admission, he had given the impression of being an average student who could either end up being a moderate academic success or a super underachiever. The Head wondered if he could be a decent bet. A more intense scrutiny of the his score cards revealed that his marks in mathematics in the All India School Certificate Examination was 95, though by the time he was writing his All India Senior School Certificate Examination two years later, they slipped to 45.

The Head 'hmm'-ed over this crucial piece of discovery and let his mind go to work. His mind replayed to him visuals of this boy who had come to meet him accompanied by his parents. The first thing that struck the Head was that the boy did look like someone who could score a 95 to raise hopes and aspirations in his parents who would then mull over this fact and encourage him to take up a course in engineering only to find that the boy could now no longer replicate that sort of high scoring success ever again.

It was a wide swing and the Head had wondered if he should place his bets on him. He reasoned that he could afford to take an occasional ambiguous student. And so, Rajib found himself enrolled in the Institute. When the semesters had started, the faculty had not reported him as a brilliant student. But then neither had he ever defaulted on attendance nor performed too badly in the exams. He seemed to have found a balance between not rising nor falling. More significantly, he had not got into any sort of mischief.

That was until recently, though.

Of late, he had begun to fall short on marks. The teachers felt that he was present in class and yet he wasn't. He looked lost in thoughts of some other place. There was no trace of him taking any interest in what was happening in the classroom. He seemed like he was wondering about things happening elsewhere. He never was absent even for a day, though. That is, until he got ran into the arms of the law.

The Head had never imagined even in his wildest dreams that Rajib would indulge in such hooliganism. He didn't seem to have it in him. It was the general belief that if a student had untoward tendencies, it would show up in everything he/she did. For example, the student would perform poorly in academics. Or at least get caught for having cheated or trying to cheat in the exams. Or be like that boy who had slapped a sleeping neighbour. But that was not the case with Rajib. Nothing of that sort happened with him.

The Head found this very interesting. This kind of a 180 degree shift in approach did not seem natural. He would have to talk to him.

He wondered what infectious influence might have distracted him in such a manner. His wonderments were cleared when Anil Thikedar had called him up to say that Rajib has been kidnapped. The Head was stunned. Who in the world was so interested in that boy so much that he had to be kidnapped?, he wondered. He himself didn't see any point in it. More stunning moments followed, when he asked the Thikedar how he had got this news. To which the Thikedar responded by saying that some rowdies who had an axe to grind with him, had done so by kidnapping Rajib who was his new lead actor.

Lead actor? Rajib?

Rajib? Lead actor?

Whenever had this happened!

The Head felt like the world around him had started to spin. He had never dealt with a kidnapping situation before. Neither had he dealt with a case where a student of his college had simultaneously achieved lead actor-ship in the local village theatre. Whatever was he going to do now? He wondered. Duty required him to ring up Rajib's parents first and inform of the fate that their son had met with, leaving the 'Lead Actor' part for a face to face discussion later. He did that, with none too constructive results. For, the parents, on their part, too, were aghast at their son's sudden unexplainable behaviour.

Adding to that, from the time they arrived at the college, there were constant accusations served out by the boy's father who was very adamant that all this was the mother's doing. 'Acting!' he had thundered. 'That too in the village theatre. And now kidnapped. My whole family's name has been ruined!' He claimed. The mother did what she was best in doing under the circumstances, which was, claim that she was only being loving and affectionate to her son while the father still held his ground obstinately and held her responsible for spoiling him.

Personally, the Head felt that the father could do a little better by asking the wife to be a little less emotional and take up a more practical approach to the matter because nothing of what they were doing helped in deciding what had to be done next.

So it was a relief when the Inspector from the Police station had called him and asked him to come and collect a boy named Rajib Deka in their custody. 'They found him! My babe!', cried the mother, shedding happy tears this time. The Head waited for Rajib's parents to come to some kind of a halt in their exchanges and outbursts so that they could all, together go to bring back Rajib.

The parents had by now, relieved by the latest news, got into debating who was to be blamed for having brought to life this brat, with the father summarily declaring that no son of his would even *think* about taking up acting. He, who hailed from a family of engineers and only engineers and that too the kind who worked only and only either in the Public Works Department or the Electricity Board or the Refineries.

'This isn't the time for any blame game.' The Head had been telling them from when they had first arrived in his office and he said that again. 'Let us first get him back', he said joining them as they went to the police station to bail out the boy.

Once back, Rajib received enough admonishments from both the parents, harshly from his father and affectionate ones from his mother, to make him sulk to great depths. He felt helpless on being asked by the disturbed parents what is it that they had not done, not given him, that he was giving them this kind of trouble? Oh, what shame he had brought to the family! Nothing of the sort had ever happened in their family in the past seven generations. Why now? Oh, why? Why, them?

Rajib did not know the answer to any of these questions. He did know something- what he had been up to and that, according to him, was not a big deal. He wanted to say, 'Hey, just chillax!' But something told him that this was not the right moment to say all that.

Meanwhile, the mother continued with her ranting. After a while, it became more than she could bear. Saying, 'I never knew I had to live to see this day', she collapsed. 'You please take some action on him as you like sir!' an angry and disheartened father told the Head.

'I want to talk to him', said the Head. There was something else going on in the Head's mind. Something which rang from what he had heard from those three pesky boys who had come the day before to tell him about Rajib's antics.

'Please go ahead.'

The Head considered the situation. It was still a complicated one. First, there was the confession from the senior boys and then there was that annoying call from that Inspector Saikia and then this call on kidnapping. Indeed, something deep and nefarious was at work and for the first time, even he had to admit that he was a little clueless on how to begin the talk. Nevertheless, talk he had to. So, after giving the matter a few minutes of thought, he began.

'Look here, this is serious.' He said. Thankfully for him, Rajib agreed. At least that is what the Head inferred from his silence. 'We are not against your choice of entertainment. But why all this violence?' He continued.

'I had only gone to watch his performance. He had said he was going to appear as twelve different characters and I wanted to see that.' For the first time, since being released, Rajib spoke.

'Okay, but why jump onto the stage and start singing?'

The boy fell silent, once again.

'Jump on stage? Singing?' Exclaimed the father sitting up straight and looking sternly at Rajib. 'You have really decided to ruin the family, is it?'

The boy cried a little before saying, 'Because he told me it was the best way to take out my anger on them. Show them who I am.'

'Who he? And who is them, now?', asked the Head wondering if there were many more were involved in this.

'He- whose buggy idea it was in the first place', said Rajib Deka with tears streaming down his cheeks. As he continued his tearful cries, he started to take off bits and pieces off him to reveal a weary Tony Baruah.

Tony Baruah!

The metamorphosis of the boy was not at all well received in the room. It made the atmosphere tense, at once. The angry Father was too shocked to react while the Head who initially had this feeling of some foul play at work, now had this uncontrollable urge to slap this fellow, resign from his job and sit at home, doors shut.

Tony Baruah!

'Rajib had asked me to become him. I thought, why not? At least that way I could give the thumbs down to some of the guys. So we got this face made from the mask maker and exchanged our faces', wept Tony. He told them of how Rajib would spend the nights rehearsing at Maharani Theatres by giving the security roll call a pass. Rajib mostly attended classes but on play days gave college a skip, leaving Tony to impersonate him.

Speaking with so much intensity after the silence made Tony feel like he was giving a speech. None in the room could believe that this impersonation plan had actually been carried out. In fact, Rajib's mother who had just recovered a little, collapsed again on finding that her son had transformed to another boy.

Tony Baruah!

The Head of the Institution recalled how it was never his intention to admit Tony to the institute in the first place. His previous academic records had spoken loudly for themselves and had convinced the Head.

'Your son should get into the fine arts.' He had advised the boy's parents and sent them away. And he sent them away four more times. But when they turned up a fifth time and that too with a recommendation from the management, he had to give in. 'This will never work', he had warned them.

Mark his words!

With Tony Baruah's recent episode of hooliganism, he had made his point. He lost no time in getting his parents called in and this time, he made his point again with facts and figures, as always.

Miserably short on attendance in all subjects of the current semester. Scored digit marks out of hundred in the recently concluded internal examination. Yet to clear the compartmental exams of all previous semesters.

'What did you expect?' The Head asked Tony's parents. They still expected him to graduate successfully from the Institute. They never had any engineers in their family before. He was going to be the first one- a son who was both an engineer and a musician. There were lots of hopes pinned on him. The Head slapped his own forehead. Whatever was the world coming to?

Meanwhile, Rajib's mother returned to her senses and quite sensibly deducted that if Tony had been masquerading as Rajib since good many days, didn't it mean that her son had been actually missing since days? In the excitement of the developments, everyone had missed this point- that Rajib Deka was *actually* kidnapped. Suddenly, the seriousness of the Thikedar's call made itself felt.

The Head found himself going back to the basics of the matter. He was already feeling cheated by being mislead by the existence two Rajib Dekas. One was bad enough in itself and two actually complicated matters. 'Oh, my god! My son, my son!' Rajib's mother uttered before her senses failed her again.

The horror of her discovery had everyone in confusion and shock. They took a few minutes to compose themselves and then, rushed off to the police station once again.

'We must hurry. No time to be lost', commanded the Head.

As they set off to the Station, Tony narrated how he and Rajib had agreed upon the identity swap for mutual benefit and how the Thikedar had made good out of it out too.

36 DINESH BARUA

Dinesh had come into the room many times before. First, as a child; then, as a teenager and subsequently, as a man. He was there in that same place that evening, yet again.

He had seen and heard all that had happened within the walls of that room. If the walls of the room could come alive or speak to him, he would have had a detailed conversation with them on those matters of the past. It would be his effort to relive those days when his father, uncles, cousins, the leaders, the officers and the many others had got together here to unite and fight the enemy. He, Dinesh, had sat through all of them. They were dangerous days.

First his father and then his two uncles escaped being killed by the thick of their skin. 'Assassination attempt', was what Dinesh had heard of it as being described as. That was sufficient for him to realize that his father was 'the man', followed by his uncles. If he was gone, all else would be gone with him too. So now there were guards, armed men about him and the uncles, and Dinesh no longer enjoyed the freedom to show up by them at those meetings at will.

Nevertheless, he was there that night in the room- this very room where he was now in- when he saw an intruder jump down into the grounds from the surrounding high walls and attack his father who was out taking an after dinner walk accompanied by his guards.

Dinesh saw his father's armed body guards fight the intruder swiftly, no sooner that another two opened a volley of unseen assaults. Hearing the shots, more armed guards arrived and made off with Dinesh's father.

Dinesh's eyes had seen one of his father's guards bump off two of the intruders and chase the remaining one. He appeared to be badly injured, limping very badly in his efforts and ultimately slumping on the ground. Dinesh was still in the room when they had brought his father in and the doctors tended to him. He knew of everything that had happened in that room since, including his father's last moments, a couple of years back.

Yet, as he stood in that room that night, he felt for the first time, that the room was holding back a secret.

He looked about the room. His eyes swept across the two sofas, the almirahs- both wooden and steel ones, the study tables, the bureau, the bed and the little table by the side of the bed. That is where his eyes came to a rest. That bed side table. He had never gone near it before. Today, it seemed to be beckoning him.

Dinesh walked up to that table and examined it. It had a drawer that was locked. He tried to open it with the few keys that he had with him. None opened it.

'What are you doing there, Dinesh da?' He turned around to find his cousin Ron standing at the door.

'That drawer is not meant to be opened', said Ron. 'You remember what *bor-deuta* had said on that?' He made a reference to Dinesh's father. 'I do', replied Dinesh going on to explain that it was not to be opened until the time was right.

'That time has come now.'

37 KOKA AGAIN

My initial elation at having found multiple trails for the missing Bharadwaj was beginning to get fizzled. Koka had presented to me the idea of there having existed at least two Bharadwajs. I had managed to track down one of them through that newspaper advert. But I couldn't do much to establish the possibility of a relationship between him and me.

The only success I had was in proving to myself that he was not likely to be alive. That however, did not qualify him in becoming my father.

Was I sad? No.

Was I disappointed? Perhaps.

Would I try again? Yes.

I had reached the dead end of one trail. But I reminded myself that I could enquire on the other one still. If it turned out that he too had died a valiant death, then I would at least have the satisfaction of knowing that irrespective of whoever of them was my father, he died a brave heart.

Encouraged by my own thoughts, I visited Koka again.

I showed him the photo of the Bharadwaj that Dinesh Barua had given me. His response was a mere 'Hmmm'. 'Bharadwaj Bordoloi is the chap I know of', he said settling back onto his chair with his hands resting on top of his walking stick that was standing between his knees.

'Any relation to the freedom fighter's family?' I asked plainly out of curiosity.

'A distant nephew I believe.'

'Bugger didn't seem to know what he was doing up there in the plane. Flew it like a bicycle with a flat tyre. Crashed immediately after take off.' I expressed my disappointment as well. After all he came from such a well known family. He should have been talented.

'Oh, he was fine, it was the other chap, the pilot.'

'Oh!!!'

'But koka, if there was a pilot, why was Bharadwaj also up there?'

'He had to be air dropped.'

'What for?'

'To scramble onto the enemy territory, something like that.'

'What!'

This sounded like some spy work. I wasn't sure I was capable of appreciating that. Nor did it make me feel any better to hear that both of them had plunged into a watery grave.

'Lake of no return?'

'Brahmaputra.'

'Brahmm---'

I was full of surprise and disappointed at the answer, instantly making me join Koka in wondering what thoughts were running in the pilot's head. 'And you radioed that news?'

'I decoded it in the telegram.'

With that the second trail also came to an end and I still gathered nothing out of it. In this case, it didn't even feel as if the Bharadwaj concerned had died a valiant death.

'Any more Bharadwajs, koka?'

'No.'

I kept looking at him. Was I expecting something more? Koka seemed to have sensed that.

'*Ma-joni*, I know at my age memory fails. But let me tell you, I remember every detail that really matters.' I smiled at that and patting him on his shoulders said, 'I trust you koka and thank you for all that help.'

38 DINESH BARUA AGAIN

I met Dinesh Barua a second time and it was at the Dunlop Hill again. Actually, it was he who insisted on the meeting. He had something more to tell me. I wondered what more he could have to say. We set the time for five in the evening of the following Friday of the week when I didn't have any lab classes to instruct.

Come Friday, I reached Dunlop Hill a little before five and occupied a table for two at the corner. I didn't want to risk being late again, something I could guarantee of myself very well since, for the past few days the chemistry teacher had been very persistently catching hold of me just as I was leaving for the day and telling me that she wasn't born yesterday, so she knew when she saw what was happening and so I should tell her whatever I knew. This highly round about strategy that she had adopted to acquire information left me feeling pretty dumb because I had no clue what she was referring too.

That is, until I was able to get away from her, reach Dunlop and sit there in peace. Then it came to me- she wanted to know what I knew of Mridu's life. 'Cheap', I muttered to myself and dropped the whole thing from my mind. A waiter came over to ask if I was going to order. I waved him off letting him know that I was expecting a guest.

Dinesh Barua came in shortly after five, carrying a folder with him. Unlike the first meeting where he appeared grounded, confident and proud of what he was sharing with me, this time he seemed to be none of those. Instead, he was speechless, restless and excited. Not to mention that he didn't know where to begin.

I ordered for a pot of tea and when it came, poured out a cup each for both of us. He was silent all along. It was only when I was nearing the finish of my cup of tea that he said the first words of the evening.

'That Bharadwaj man', he started 'was a brave heart.' I, of course, agreed, having clear recollection of the man's actions, as narrated by Barua himself. He took a sip and paused before saying, 'He didn't die'. He said it to no one in particular, as if he were making a general announcement. For sure, this surprised me.

Having defied death, he was just badly injured and had collapsed when Barua had last seen him. The Barua family ever so grateful to the man for his services paid for his travel to Guwahati and his treatment over there.

'But there was a problem', he said, this time looking at me.

The man had seen something of grave importance on the night of the attack- the face of the third attacker who had got away. When he was able to recollect it to the police and later the army, it gave them the first hope of getting closer to the mastermind behind these attacks. If they could keep up the trail, they might reach the Chief as well.

But they also realized that Bharadwaj was in danger. The danger of having been the only person to be alive after being injured in a fight with the mastermind's band.

It was not something that the Chief of the enemy would care to forgive and forget. It would, in all likelihood, make him redesign his plans to include the killing of this man before going ahead with anything else.

'So we killed Bharadwaj before that could happen.'

'What!'

I was shocked. How could they do this to the very man they had saved?

'There was no other option.' He told me proceeding further to extract an old paper clipping from his file folder. It was a news report in Assamese that carried the details of how a young guard named Bharadwaj had died as he fought off the assassins of Hiten Baruah, the well known tea planter. There was Bharadwaj's photo and that of his funeral pyre as well with the story around it.

I was disappointed, disgusted and pained all at the same time. Was this what Dinesh Baruah had called me for? To listen to how they had carried out murder?

'This is so…so…', I cried unable to say more for want of the right word.

'Fake.' Baruah interjected.

'What?'

'This was fake. A fake death and a fake funeral.'

I didn't trust that. I didn't say anything either. I didn't even look at him. I just stared on the floor trying to calm myself down. Barua noticed none of these. He had, by now got rid of his restlessness and was thoroughly excited. 'It was the army who had strategized this.' He said. 'They saw an advantage here.'

The strategy here being, to convince the enemy that they had nothing to get on the trail of their Chief by 'killing Bharadwaj' and sending out the 'proof'. And then, from the ashes of that fake funeral would rise a new person whose destiny it would be to crawl into the enemy territory and be a mole. While operatives of this mission would know him as Agent Decode, he would be officially known to everyone as Captain Bharadwaj Bordoloi.

'And that Bharadwaj Bordoloi died on the way when his plane crashed into the Brahmaputra.' I said.

'No.'

But that was what koka had told me and in that moment I trusted koka's words more than Dinesh's.

'The plane crashed- yes. The pilot died- yes. Bharadwaj did not.'

'Don't tell me he swam across the flooded Brahmaputra and walked into the enemy territory.'

The last person to do that was the Srimanta Sankardev and that was in the fifteenth century. Subsequent attempts have proved to be fatal. A flooded Brahmaputra is no joke. It is mighty ferocious for God's sake!

Dinesh Barua admitted that while he could not explain this, nevertheless the truth was that Bharadwaj indeed reached his destination and did proceed with his intelligence gathering because he had communicated with his army team.

Barua opened his folder and this time took out envelopes filled with letters and placed them before me. 'These are the duplicate extracts', he said. 'Ok' I uttered, not in the least interested in examining them.

Dinesh Barua went on to narrate how the resurrected Bharadwaj who had made his way into the enemy territory had begun discovering their step-by-step plans of weakening the defence mechanism of the state and sent coded messages to his team. Hitesh Baruah's estates benefited much from them. For a few months all went according to the plan. But when attack after attack began to fail, doubts began to creep in. A wounded enemy that finds itself spied upon is most ruthless. But Captain Bharadwaj Bordoloi held his honour, until his last breath. His lifeless body was sighted at an isolated segment of the wired fencing along his motherland by a patrol unit.

A few hours later on that same day, violence erupted at the Merapani bazaar turning it into an unlikely battlefield that left hundreds dead and thousands homeless.

'That is when he finally died', concluded Dinesh Barua.

'And this time we buried him.' As if doing anything else was going to bring him back to life, like in the earlier instance.

'Lake of No Return?'

'War cemetery.'

'Where is that?'

'Near the Lake of No Return.'

And all the while I thought I had learnt everything about the lake.

39 AUNT SARAH'S TRUTH

As far as I was concerned, I believed that I had spent my evening tea time listening to some dramatic action packed war time spying activities. I had learnt of how one Bharadwaj had morphed into another by pretending to be dead, before dying for real finally. And where had that left me? Nowhere.

None of these provided any evidence of heredity.

I made up my mind that neither of these Bharadwajs suited to be my father. That whichever uncle wrote that letter must have been going through senile decay while doing so thinking how very funny of him; that the 'B' in my name was destined to remain a mystery forever and that Mr. James Brendon was my father whether anyone liked it or not.

This was so much easier to live with. It allowed me to go about my work- invigilating exams, evaluating course work and other mundane stuff.

We had reached the end of the semester and that meant examinations were around the corner. It was not necessary that I went to college every day. But I did. After this investigation saga on the Bharadwajs, it proved to be a relaxant. As I sat in the Dr B.N Saikia Lab, I didn't do much work. But in the company of others I could keep myself engaged in conversations with them. In doing so, I found a sort of relief from my anger and disappointment. Then, there was the occasional student who showed up to clear 'doubts'.

In this tumultuous time, Sudhir and Nandita were in particular very understanding of my situation and did their best to help me stay positive. Initially it was a little awkward for both of them when they had read the newspaper story on my fathers. How did one react to that sort of news? I told them the problem wasn't that I had *fathers*. At least it was not *my* problem. My problem was that, me having two fathers seemed to bother some other staff members- the maths teacher in particular- who had now taken to giving me a weird look that told me that she was having difficulty in deciding which compartment of her brain should she put me in.

That was kind of discomforting. Especially when this dilemma in her head caused her to start muttering under her breath and then join up with whoever else was around, all the while giving me guarded looks. That's where Sudhir and Nandita were most helpful. They always made it a point to ensure that I was accompanied by either of them so that any uncomfortable talk, should it pop up, could be easily diverted. Meanwhile the Ph.D holders of the department had jointly declared that 'this is life.' Since I too had not missed this point, by and large we got along as harmoniously as earlier.

Also, I spent more time in the company of the tea-lady who felt much kindness towards me, comforting me with her tea and stock of snacks. Having been raised by three different mothers and now living with her second husband and four children, she understood my situation. She did her best by sharing all the gossip she had heard. Especially, all the talk in the air about the two boys doing some sort of mischief that landed one in the police station and got another kidnapped. Somehow I sensed humour in this and the episode cheered me up. Perhaps it was providing me with a kind of emotional support- that I was not alone in search for my identity. Gradually, I got back to my normal living.

Then one morning, Aunt called up. She wanted to meet me. 'Haven't seen you in a while', she claimed. This was true. Ever since I had arrived at the Institute, I had not gone to visit her. She was supposed to have come on the day of Varun's visit which also did not materialize. But we did talk and she was aware of my father tracking efforts.

She arrived shortly after ten in the morning. I walked her around the campus showing her the various developments that had build up since she had brought me here for the interview. The swimming pool, for instance. Along the way we met a couple of fellow professors with whom we exchanged pleasantries and then came to my quarters.

'Your bag of goodies, Gigglepot.' She said with a mischievous grin, once we were in. She knew very well that it was her cookies and cakes that I always had my eyes on. She never failed to get box loads of them ready when I came visiting or like in this case, when it was her visiting me. There were also some letters from Amy and magazines from Eddie that I had asked for.

I grinned back.

Gigglepot.

That was what daddy thought I was- giggling forever. He had gone on to declare that when I was born, unlike other babies who cried their lungs out, I had giggled till my sides ached. Even the doctors were puzzled and he claimed that there were stories of them slapping my tiny body in efforts to get me cry. But all I would still do is giggle. He was convinced that I had a secret pot of giggles boiling somewhere inside me that produced all those giggles and so even decided that I should be named Gigglepot Brendon. But then Aunt interfered and ensured that I had a nice official name. However, for all un-official reasons, I remained Gigglepot, even if I wasn't a Brendon anymore. But then neither was I giggling anymore of late.

'You've become the talk of the town, huh?' She teased me about the newspaper stories on my search for my 'other' father, pulling my cheeks. 'Oh, come on, auntie, not you!'

'Why not? After all I am your aunt'. That was pretty heartfelt. I smiled back.

For some reason, having Aunt around that day felt like a déjà vu. Something similar to when she had come visiting me shortly after Dad's funeral. Then, I had supposed that she wanted to discuss something – family matters. The sort that elderly relatives like to talk about when they feel that the bereaved person is now ready to take it on. I despise such discussions and therefore, was not too welcoming of her. Fortunately, there was no such talk. We chatted for a while, had tea and then, Aunt left.

I wondered if that talk was going to happen now. If it was, I didn't see it coming as yet. We prepared ourselves a short lunch and retired for a siesta afterwards. When we were up by tea time, Aunt suggested that we go out.

'Some place where we can sit and talk.'

'Oh-ho, ok. How about Dunlop Hills?'

'Sounds good!'

So Dunlop Hills, it was.

Evening had just set in and the place was not yet crowded. But not wanting to take a chance of running into fellow Ayotics, I decided it would be better to sit in a relatively secluded area of the place. So there we were sitting in a table for two set up with glasses of orange juice in front of us. If Aunt Sarah was going to do any Big Talk, we were all set for it.

We were doing general chit chat and looking through the menu card at the table as I recounted my earlier visits here to the Dunlop Hills. At the end of it there was a brief pause in our conversation after which said Aunt, 'You know, I knew your mother.'

My jaws dropped at that. I mean, of course she would know my mother. After all she was the one who had fixed the marriage of my mother with her brother. What was the big deal in that?

'Right.' That was the only response that I could think of.

'Exactly.'

Looked like round one of a 'talk' was done with. I had a feeling that I could now see the actual talk coming in.

'As in, I knew your mother before she became your mother'. This looked like another ice breaking statement since it was uttered with more smiles along with some moist-y eye contact. So the only reply I could think of in response was an 'uh-huh?' But thankfully, after that, words actually began to flow freely.

'Your mother and I used to work together. We were both nurses at the State Hospital.'

Now, *that* was something I had never known. Until then, I had known my mother to be only a house wife and someone who was forever pulling my ears.

40 THE HOSPITAL

It was a cold winter night. All was quiet around the Government Hospital and inside too. Except at the emergency ward. It was that place where alertness had firmly fixed its existence. Embodied in person of the Chief Nurse, it was ever ready to manage any crisis that would rise. This alertness and silence of the night was disturbed by the noiseless arrival of the hospital ambulance.

It had only its light on, not the siren. The back door of the van opened and two armed men jumped out. After quickly inspecting the ward, they signaled to the occupants inside to come out. A man was brought out. He was severely wounded and covered in blood, having taken in many bullets. It was a wonder that he was even alive.

After being operated upon, he was put into an isolated ward. Those two armed men guarded him. Except for the doctors and nurses who had attended to him first, no one else was allowed to even as much have a peep at him.

He was special; the armed men had told the Chief Nurse. He was special because there were people after him who would want to kill him but that could not be allowed. He had seen the face of the enemy! That mastermind! They would want to know if he was dead and if not, to make him dead. But he could not be allowed to die. He was needed.

The Chief Nurse was not so sure of her new patient. Only a miracle would save him, she felt. And the miracle did happen. After many weeks, her patient sat up. A few more, and he was walking a little. Some more and he was able to take a leisurely stroll in the garden of the hospital under the eyes of the Nurse- In Charge- she, who had tended to him since he was first admitted. Those armed men were not going to loosen their guard.

Then one day, a couple of plainclothesmen came and escorted him and his two armed guards onto a jeep and left. The chief nurse later came to know that those plainclothesmen were from the army.

A month later, the Nurse- In-Charge came rushing in with a newspaper in her hand. She was sobbing inconsolably. 'He's dead!' She shrieked pointing to a news report in the paper that she was carrying. 'They got him!'

The Chief Nurse had a look at that- it was her former patient! For a moment, she too turned speechless in shock. 'But we did what we could' She tried to console her nurse. But it didn't make her feel any good.

Oh, why did it have to be this way?, she asked.

When she was due a baby, their baby.

Baby!

The word hit her like a bolt from the blue. And yet…yet, it gave her a strange feel of familiarity. As if it was she and not her nurse who was going through this … like an old piece of memory that had been tucked away in the deep interiors of the mind had suddenly jerked free and come alive.

Ah, yes…yes… it felt exactly like that. The memory seemed to be replaying itself. But there was a difference. She had been mourning the loss of her third baby on being told of her husband's death in an insurgents' attack. It was all wrong. She knew it then and she knew it now too. She also knew that she had to do something about it. In front of her was the weeping figure of the young nurse. Placing an assuring hand on her shoulder, she led her away…

Deftly done paperwork had the nurse shifted from the State Hospital to the Garden Hospital at the Duroni Tea Estate, while she herself escorted the nurse to the place. Her brother had come to receive them at the station. It was no coincidence that he was also the Supervisor of the estate, having taken up after his father. James Brendon had displayed a flair for this quite early in life.

Post dinner, leaving the nurse to rest in her room, James and Sarah sat down for a talk. It was mostly Sarah speaking, James listening. 'But Sarah…' said James, when she had finally had her say. But Sarah would not listen. The way she saw it, James had nothing to lose. He had already lost his missus.

The conversation left me in frenzy. 'Come back with me.' I told Aunt. 'I have something to show you'. We went back to my quarters. The route seemed unusually longer this time. When we finally reached, I opened the door frantically and rushed into my room to get the photo that Dinesh Barua had given me.

Aunt followed me wondering what had got into me. I put the photo in her hands and asked her if this was the same man she was talking about.

'That's him', she said as calmly as she could and looked at me. I smiled and a few minutes later uttered a most idiotic, 'Wow!'

It felt like I had successfully come to the end of a chase and I had won. That seemed to have made me happy. But I found my Aunt crying and she kept on saying that there was no need for all this. I assured her that it was alright. It wasn't anybody's fault. She had been helping her friend and that was really okay.

Besides it was a happy ending, both then and now. So why cry? But she kept crying and saying 'You don't understand. It was all very difficult and that was not needed.'

Now, this was indeed something that I really did not understand and I also could not figure out what 'need' was she referring to. As far as I was concerned, I had found the answers to my questions and despite that, everything was as it had always been.

Yet, my Aunt, did not seem to feel any better. But after sleeping the night over and after an enthusing cup of ginger tea and toast the next morning, her spirits were back when she went home.

41 MY TRUTH

The last time I had had such an 'adult' and 'serious' conversation with Aunt Sarah was when I had met her at Dad's funeral. But it was nowhere as revealing as the most recent one that I had just had. My thoughts went back to that day.

Dad was buried on a normal, bright morning. Nothing about it was particularly mournful. Not even the thought that I was not there at those last moments when he had said, 'Gigglepot, always read', filled me with grief. Read, I always did. When I did not, he used to read to me. I am not sure how much I enjoyed those reading sessions; but for some reason I felt that, his eyes were filled with gratitude every time I let him read to me.

Earlier that morning, prior to my arrival, there had been some debate regarding the conduct of the final rites. There were some people who said that since he had become 'one of us', he should be carried to the grounds for cremation. Sheer nonsense, I thought. I could even hear Dad say that.

Even though he had settled in the country, he was still a 'firangi', a foreigner. But being married to my Mother, who was a 'desi', native, perhaps he too was 'desi' enough? Having predeceased her husband, mother had things easy. Dad was clear that all rites and rituals would be as per her faith. Since that is how she had come about into the family. Much like their wedding.

Aunt's bizarre request had indeed put her brother in one kind of fix. But he had agreed. So now he had to set about doing it all right. He knew that this marriage was going to be about acceptance and creating a lot of that.

Having no precedence to follow on, he sought the guidance of the priest in the nearby church. The priest, an Englishman himself, was plain dismissive of the suggestion that Dad made to him - a two religion joint wedding. But then, neither was Dad the kind of man to be bogged down by a 'No'.

Without much ado, he managed to procure a Hindu priest at short notice who, though a little reluctant at first, eventually agreed to conduct a quick ritual to declare them man and wife, seeing that it was the only way to end the situation. So, James Brendon in his coat, tie and a crown of Indian Basil flowers on his head, sat cross legged in front of the Holy Fire and a banana sapling surrounded by earthen lamps, waiting for his veiled bride to arrive and sit next to him so that they could take the wedding vows.

It was definitely a private affair with only his best friend Bill and his wife in attendance, though even they were not told the details leading to the marriage. It was *that* private. However, it was not at all a grave occasion, the happiness factor being ushered in by the women workers from the tea estate who danced and sang wedding songs and gave out the *uruli*, a blessed omen given by a long sequence of ululating sound- when the ceremony was completed. Later in the evening, Dad had given a lavish feast to all the workers in the estate.

Likewise were her final rites. Though Dad did not, rather, was not given a role to play. The relatives from her side arrived, carried her to the pyre and lit it. The last he saw of her was when she was being taken away, dressed in her bridal finery, complete with the vermillion in her hair parting, a sign that she had left behind a husband. They didn't ask him how he felt nor offer any condolences.

Again, not to be left wanting in ensuring his wife's soul made an easy entry into the astral world; Dad let the lamp stay lit in the room where she breathed her last, until the cremation was over. Later, on the twelfth and final day of mourning, he arranged for some pooja and fed a few priests, orphans and made donations to them.

That was much better than what I had to go through. I was just a dumb spectator, occasionally following instructions. Like when I had to go around the pyre behind my uncle while he 'broke the pot of water' and poured the fire. Nobody spoke to me. Everything was conveyed in gestures.

I had my cheeks wet with tears. Though, I did not know if the tears were more from the flaming fire or the broken feelings hard to bear within. I felt separated. No, I *was* separated. Mother was now gone. Dad, Aunt, Eddie and Amy were all ordered to remain at the gates of the crematorium. And the people around me were all watching me as if I was some kind of a show piece put on display. 'She's the daughter', I heard them say to one another in hushed tones.

After the funeral, I went along with them to their home for the customary twelve day mourning period. Over the 'hobis'- rice boiled with vegetables and salt- I met many who were in the first line of connection but distanced by my mother having 'broken' caste and religion. But there was no warmth in these meetings. In that time, I found a shell of invisibility building around me, as if shielding me from the world.

A shell that toughened me up to not betray any emotion.
A shell within which I could feel safe when alone.
A shell that remained with me ever since.

On the thirteenth day, when the priest said his prayers and sprinkled holy water over all of us declaring us 'free' from the 'pollution' caused by the death, I was sent back. There were no offers to stay in touch. Instead, I was instructed to give away all of my mother's possessions so that her soul would not be trapped in its attachment for those.

With Dad, there was much argument for which I saw no reason. If mother had followed her faith, Dad would follow his. I made the announcement that Aunt Sarah would decide. So she did. Sure there were people around. But none of them were from Mother's side.

People around me were talking. Rather, they were wondering how I was taking it. Whereas I was wondering how we were all taking it- Aunt, Eddie, Amy and I. He was all that we had as a father figure, a guide.

But the focus was more on me. Seeing no reaction from me, there was a general assumption that I was not as 'affected' as I should have been. After all, there was very little about me that they could claim was very 'firangi'. My accent, my upbringing and now, the coldness with which I was bidding farewell to Dad. That was all to my list of 'firangi-ness'. But it was this third 'trait' that seemed particularly 'firangi' to them.

I knew better.

Though not numbed by grief, I was aware of the feeling surging in me. It was a feeling that finally, a strange relationship has come to an end. The relationship that bound -Dad, Mother and Me.

Dad was the outgoing, fun loving, living in the moment type – trying out new things and getting excited over every little thing that I did. But strangely forever falling shy of getting Mother to join him in his endeavors. Mother on the other hand, never opposed his doings nor did she have anything of her own to suggest. The response always being, 'If it is ok with you, it's fine with me too.'

I once tried to get her to oppose Dad, just for the fun of it. She was alarmed by the idea. But apart from that, there was no other reaction. At moments like these, I felt that we were strangers who were trying to bond like a family.

I could have explored this possibility, of course. Unfortunately, I was sent off to boarding school. From there on, started the time, when I was a visitor to my own home. Even during those visits, I found little improvement in our relationship.

Then, with Dad and Mother passing away, it had started to become a thing of past. My thoughts then returned to the day I read the letter which Dad had wrote to me in his last hours.

'Dear Gigglepot', it had begun.

As I went through the letter in my mind, all over again, I once again lived through all of those emotions that never had a chance to express itself, until that day.

The suddenness of my long hidden suspicion coming true- that I had been brought up by my step- Dad; the meaning of the strangeness in the family; of the silence which no one ever wanted to break; of the pain in forgetting secrets because they were supposedly buried.

As I sat in my room, I wondered what it must have been like for Aunt Sarah to ask her brother to take Bharadwaj's place so that her nurse and the unborn child may live; what must have James Brendon felt, when he had to hold in his arms a baby that was not his but yet be its father and to give it his name and it certainly must have been shattering for mother to accept a new man for a husband since the father of her unborn child was dead.

But this was the script that Providence had written and it had to be complied with. It required grieving for one man and wedding with another in the winter that followed after the war had ended. The following fall, I arrived in a bundle for Mrs. & Mr. Brendon.

42 BUSTED!

Just because Inspector Saikia's brilliance had never been appreciated nor condemned, it did not mean that he was dumb. He had his brains intact and was confident that sooner or later he would get the chance to do it some justice. With the present set of cases involving kidnapping, missing persons and arrests, he felt that, the time had indeed finally come.

He had felt something amiss from the time that he had received the Thikedar's phone call which came just after he had finished speaking to the Principal of the Technical Institute to whom he informed that he had Rajib Deka locked up in the police station. Because, one thing was pretty improbable- you could not kidnap a fellow and simultaneously put him in a police lock up. But it seemed that with Rajib Deka this was not only probable, it was a certainty. Common sense made Saikia to doubt if, there were two people by the same name studying in the same institute.

It was at this juncture of his thinking that the Principal of the Institute of Technical Education and his retinue turned up at the police station.

'Please find our son!', wailed Rajib's father seriously considering the possibility of what would befall the world and what all it would be deprived of should this engineer gem of a son not be found. For a moment Saikia had thought he had a new case in hand and was alarmed that all of a sudden so many people had gone missing. It was an unnatural statistic for Imranpur. But, on a closer look at the people assembled, he realized that he had met them before. In fact, a very short while ago.

'You are back again!' He exclaimed.

'Our son has been kidnapped', said Rajib's father. 'Yes, sir. He has been kidnapped. Please find him!', cried another voice which turned out to be Rajib's mother. Apparently, she had decided that she would not be left behind in the search for her son. So the moment she came back to her senses, she too made a dash to the police station accompanied by Sudhir who could be relied to be a Man Friday on such situations.

'Details please?'
'Rajib Deka of Institute of Technical Education.'
'What? Didn't you come here and bail him out?', asked the annoyed Inspector.

'Oh yes, that boy. This is who he turned out to be. This boy-Tony Baruah.' Rajib's father continued his woeful tale, pointing at Tony. This was something that Saikia was not familiar with. How could one boy transform into another?

At this strategic moment, the Principal of the Institute of Technical Education told the bewildered Saikia about the 'Tony Baruah being dressed up as Rajib Deka' episode. Okay, agreed Saikia. That meant, he would have to search for Rajib, he figured.

An investigator trained in the school of orderly arrangement of thoughts, he tried to put the facts in a logical fashion before embarking on a rescue mission. If, Rubul is missing; the kidnapper's have Rubul yet the Thikedar claims the kidnappers have Rajib Deka and not Rubul and the locked up Rajib Deka has morphed into another boy called Tony Baruah, that means some foul play is at work. What this practically translated to, was that Saikia continued to be clueless on- where is Rajib Deka and Rubul Kalita?

A most annoying discovery to make. He sat surrounded by this crowd of people, not knowing what to do while the people looked expectedly towards him for the next course of action. After some intense thinking, he got clarity on what he had to do next - nab the kidnappers who had either Rubul or Rajib in their custody.

The question that now remained was – how.

Just then, Saikia's subordinate came running in. In the absence of a separate cyber crime section, Saikia himself had to look after it and since Imry was not exactly making a name for itself in this arena, he had delegated the task to his subordinate. So it was that this man got the job of tracing the origin of the email which the kidnappers had sent to the Thikedar.

'Sir!' He exclaimed.

'Sir! That email has been traced to Hari Om Intarnate Café, sir!' He spoke triumphantly.

'It comes from an email account of a Bikash Kumar.'

'Wonderful!', complimented Saikia on the good work.

'What email?', asked the Head. Saikia explained the state of things.

'Oh no, my son has been kidnapped over internet!', concluded Rajib's mother before succumbing to another round of hysterics. Nobody had time to attend to this, not even the ever patient Sudhir who had a knack of calming down hysterical people and before she could take it to her head to ask if 'internet detectives' were needed to be hired to track her son, the party got onto a waiting jeep and set off to Hari Om Intarnate Café.

'Wait', cautioned the Head just as they were about to get off the jeep after reaching the computer café. 'What now?' Saikia wanted to know. He was getting impatient to finish this irritating business. 'You think this Bikash Kumar character will simply give away like that?', the Head asked. He had a point there. Rajib's parents could now see why this man was respected for being strategic.

'I will pick him up for interrogation and then, all shall be revealed,' said Saikia. 'You really think it will be as simple as that?' The Head wanted to know. This caused a doubt to arise in Saikia's mind. It had never happened before simply because no other case had been as taxing as this.

'So what do you propose we do?', asked Saikia acknowledging that, indeed the plan should be more specific to meet the objective.

The Head suggested that he would go in and initiate a conversation, while the others stayed back and observed. How that conversation would be manipulated to reveal more about Rajib or Rubul's whereabouts would be left to the Head. He was confident that he could do this. He was also confident that he could break the morale of whoever was behind this, during the course of the conversation that would subsequently lead to some sort of scuffle. It would be then that Saikia and his men could arrive at the scene.

Saikia agreed that this was a better plan. Accordingly, the group split up- The Head, Saikia and the constables on one jeep and the affected parents in the safe company of Sudhir, in another. Thus, they moved on.

'Good evening, brother!', greeted the Head as he arrived at the entrance of the café.

'Yes?', came a rude reply from the other end.

'I am the Head of the engineering college over here.'

'So? You can be anybody. Why bother me?'

Clearly, this man was not a friendly one.

'Why I am bothering you, you will come to know. For now, let us get onto business. Do you know of any Bikash Kumar?'

'What makes you think I do?'

'Because he certainly seems to know you'. This perplexed the man.

'What? How?'

'He came to your café and sent a mail from one of your machines.'

'Many people come here and send mails. Do you expect me know them all?'

The conversation had now come to a point where all friendliness in the Head had vanished and the stern straight talker had raised its head.

'Well, that email claimed that he- Bikash- had kidnapped our hero of the village theatre', said the Head. He further went on to say that the police had found out that the email had been sent from here and hence were on the lookout. So, if Hari Om Intarnate Café' did not cooperate, the police would have to take some action.

Since Imry was a small place, everyone knew everyone directly or indirectly, in one way or the other. So, this was a threat worth giving out to the man. It worked. Fear rose in the man's eyes as he mumbled that, indeed, he knew Bikash. In fact, he had employed him. Hearing this, the Head told the man to call Bikash. Simultaneously, he turned around to signal to Saikia to be on alert. They would need to jump into action at any moment.

The police force did not have to wait for long.

When Bikash turned up by his employer's side, he was conveyed the reason for this sudden summons. This gave him the jitters. The police jeep and van waiting a short distance away did not miss his attention either. 'Is it really you?', he was being repeatedly asked by both his boss and the Head. But he was too numb to answer. He merely stood rooted to the spot with his head down and his eyes shifting from here to there and from the Head to the Café Owner.

Gradually, waking up to the reality of the situation, he got a grasp over himself. He realized that the longer he stayed back in the presence of these two men, the harder the interrogation would become. So it made sense to get away from there at the earliest. This, he understood, was going to be a difficult task. But since it was the only way out, he was going to do it.

In the flash of a second, Bikash slumped to the floor and pushing asides the legs of his employer and the alien interrogator, wiggled his way out from the café. He was now out on the road, running. It took the Head and the Café Owner a few minutes to recover from the blows they had received below their knees. Once back up on their feet, the Head delivered another wave at which Saikia with his men got into the pursuit. Caught by the spirit of the things and smarting from Bikash's hits, the Café Owner and the Head doubled their enthusiasm and energy to join the rest of the people that included Sudhir and the parents of the two boys along with Tony. The police, of course, had the lead but only till the point that Bikash was within their line of sight.

The roads in Imry were not wide. In fact, they were so narrow, that at a time either a vehicle or a man could occupy it for movement. To add to that, the criss-crossing of the roads often meant that a newcomer to the area had the possibility of going around in circles before realizing that they were actually heading nowhere.

That is what was happened to the 'Bikash Chasers'. They were heavily losing out against Bikash.

Being a local, Bikash knew his way around fluently, a distinct disadvantage that the others had. Their only consolation was that they had the café owner with them, who, with his sporadic directions that consisted of 'he's off to the fields!', 'this way now', did a good job of directing the party of chasers to be always within their target's range.

However, Bikash was still leading.

He had jumped over the compound wall of a house thinking he could disappear along the road behind it. But it was a badly calculated move. For, he had jumped into the grounds of another house, landing right in the middle of a pack of geese that was bustling about. The disturbed geese fluttered about in panic while Bikash struggled to get his hold back to be on the run. When he gathered himself up, he made for the gate of the house to reach out to the road again. By now, even he got confused as to where he actually was. But not wasting time to think on that, he started running.

His momentum pushed him past the gates, breezing on to the road where the blaring of a horn caught him by surprise and brought him to a sudden stand still.

The horn blared from a Magic. Bhupen's Magic. Sitting inside it was Bhupen himself and me. I was returning from a visit to koka to update him of the turn of events that had happened since we had last met.

'Bikash!', exclaimed Bhupen.

'Bhupen da!' Bikash returned the recognition.

These were some of the additional privileges of being in the public transportation service- one also became acquainted with the loafers. 'Let me in', said Bikash and without waiting for a response, he pushed himself into the rear seat of the Magic. 'Go now, hurry!', he urged. Bhupen felt a little lost at this sudden set of activities but managed to get the vehicle going. However, hardly had we moved a few feet, we were brought to a halt by another vehicle.

It was a jeep. A police jeep. That too, Saikia's.

Saikia peered out of his jeep and spotting us, screamed at his cousin. 'Bhupen, I did not expect this from you! You are helping a criminal!' A shocked Bhupen yelled back a No and turning to Bikash shouted, 'You liar, you… you..how *dare* you!'

But Bikash had no time for such exchanges or explanations. Jumping out of the Magic, he started running in the opposite direction. Saikia, his constables and the rest of the members of the chasing party that had caught up by now, all got off their jeeps and started running after Bikash. 'I'll see you later on this', I heard Saikia grunt to Bhupen as he got past him.

After Saikia dashed off, we saw Sudhir and his party of parents show up. 'Sudhir!' I exclaimed. 'What's happening?' I asked. 'We are chasing the kidnapper.' He informed. 'The kid-what?' I was bewildered at what I heard.

'Come *ma-joni*, let us give them a hand', said Bhupen rising to the occasion. Besides, he had to shed off the false impression that Saikia had picked up about him that he was providing safe passage to criminals in Imry. Not wanting to be left behind, we too set off.

The game of chasing had by now come to a point where Bikash was running on a one way road with houses on either side. He could now, only be caught. Any other outcome was not foreseeable. Encouraged by this deduction, everyone doubled their efforts. But semi intelligent that the fellow was, he pulled a totally unexpected act- he jumped to the roof of a house. Racing up to the top of the roof, from where he could be seen from several meters, he shouted, 'If anyone of you come any closer, I will jump off from here. Did you hear me? I will jump off!'

Now, this was something no one had expected.

'What do we do now?', asked a baffled Saikia to the Head. The Head, in turn, took off his specs and with a rather disgusting expression admitted that indeed, for the moment even he was dumbfounded. 'Let us wait.' Saikia suggested. The Head nodded. It seemed to be the best thing to do for the moment. Besides, it also gave everybody time to think of the next move.

And so, the wait began. The sun set and the moon rose ushering in the night fall. By now, news of the chase that ended with the culprit getting perched on the roof top and that of his threat, had spread through the village; the owner of the house on whose roof Bikash had taken refuge being the informer. 'Shut up!' Saikia had shouted at him but it was too late by then. He had feared that spreading the news might cause the partners in crime to take action elsewhere. If that happened, Saikia's policing instincts told him, that, it would lead to breakdown of law and order. It could also mean bombs suddenly making itself present. And bombs were the last things Saikia wanted at the moment.

Darkness had also set in. Being devoid of street lights in the vicinity, we had to rely on battery operated torches of all shapes and sizes as well as the occasional kerosene lamps when the torches went out, to keep a vigil at the site.

This tense and highly excitable atmosphere gradually began to turn a little relaxed when the passing by balloon and sweet seller to whom it appeared as if some new form of street entertainment was on show, decided to set up their stalls, wanting to make some business out of it. But finding that the tension of such a situation was getting diffused by their presence, Saikia ordered his men to chase them off.

Bikash turned out to be a rather stubborn criminal. He simply would not budge from the place. He squatted at the roof top, hurling abuses and threats alternately whenever the police or anyone else tried any form of negotiation or persuasion with him. We knew of the latest position that Bikash had assumed every time a light beam that fell on him, blinded him, making him swear profusely. Other times, we guessed his position by following the glowing orange light of his bidi that traced half arcs in the air as it moved to and away from his lips.

It definitely looked like a deadlock situation. We had almost come to think that only divine intervention could rescue us from this when we heard a sudden thud, an inhuman howl and an equally indecent mewing. This was quickly followed by a few people from the gathering shouting, 'He's fallen, he's fallen!' It was sufficient to get the crowd and the police run to the spot. 'Quick! We cannot lose him a second time!' Saikia was heard giving orders to his team as they all ran to catch him.

The whole incident had such a tremendous appeal of interest that even though I was unaware of who the police were after and why, I still wanted to be around and see what was happening. So I stood there, quite a distance from the actual scene of this final scuffle. As I was trying to make the most of it, I heard a familiar voice greet me from behind.

'Hello, *ma-joni!*'

I turned around only to find that it was Koka, carrying Aditi on one hand, grinning with satisfaction. Something about his grin made me suspect him that he had hand in ensuring Bikash's fall. 'Don't tell me.. it was Aditi up there,' I told him. 'Of course she was up there!' Koka confirmed my suspicion.

Having heard of the incident, Koka too had come to see what was happening. But soon he was tired of Bikash's prank. So Koka decided to take matters in his own hands. He sent Aditi up on the roof and set her after him. Aditi also played up to the spirit of things. Given that Bikash was at the mercy of the darkness, he ended up getting stalked by the cat and the final straw came when she pounced on him. Well, well, koka had every right to help Saikia!

I offered to walk koka back to his house but Bhupen accompanied him back. So I decided to stay back and find out more.

In the mean time, Saikia and his men returned to their jeeps carrying a bundled up Bikash with them, accompanied by the rest of the chasing party. They got into the other jeep and I managed to squeeze myself in between, as we made our way back to the police station.

Once we reached the station, Bikash's interrogation began. Therein, his inexperience in committing crimes showed when, after a rather short round of not-so-harsh-questioning, Bikash revealed the empty house where he had sheltered the kidnapped prize. A rather lame surrender, observed Saikia, but better than running after a cow, he noted. This was worth it. Thereafter, there was little searching to be done.

Bikash and his gang still had their captured shadow under the wraps. Their horror knew no bounds when they unwrapped their 'Return Gift' in front of the police, the Principal, Tony Baruah and the boys' parents.

It was Rajib Deka.

The men in uniform lost no time in rounding up Bikash and his side kicks who were hauled up by Saikia's men like sitting ducks, while Rajib's father caught hold of him only to give him one tight slap. 'That will teach you how to have fun, you boy!', the father admonished the son. Perhaps it would have continued to some more extent but for the Head's intervention.

Rounding up the convicts in the police lock up, the party split up. While the students returned to their college along with us - that included the Principal, Sudhir, myself and parents; the policemen went back to the Station happy to have had a good catch but in no mood to think of what became of Rubul Kalita. The two boys on the other hand, wondered what would become of them.

In the meanwhile, I found a relatively calm moment to whisper into Sudhir's ears that I had seen these two boys at the Dunlop Hills one recent Saturday afternoon talking about plans and money to Sarat and another man who might have been the owner. Sudhir gave me a look that was both full of shock and astonishment at once.

43 CALLING THE BLUFF

Sudhir had found himself in many awkward situations before during his time in the college. Like the time when his colleague and friend from the college Debhargya had fainted upon being told that a boy in the hostel whose warden he was, was in the process of attempting suicide using a gamusa. So while the rest of the male staff including the Dean, Hostel Supervisor and Principal stood circling the boy telling he was being comical and nonsensical and hence should stop it immediately, Sudhir found himself rushing Debhargya to a doctor who was most annoyed at being woken up in the middle of the night to treat a man of delicate spirits who was otherwise perfectly healthy.

Then, there was the time when he had come face to face with Nandita, his junior in ASEC for whom he always had nursed tender feelings but had never taken an action on them. He found it extremely awkward to be colleagues with her at work. Thankfully, he was able to solve this problem by confessing about it to her on the bus ride back to home from college.

But by far the most awkward thing he had ever done till date was waking up on a Sunday morning and deciding that THIS was the day for him to walk up to Nandita's father and ask for his daughter's hand in marriage. He had not fancied that he would be waking up to such thoughts when he had gone to sleep the previous night.

However, none of these prepared him for the awkwardness that had showed up at the entrance of the Dr B. N Saikia lab that late evening, in the form of Mridu. For the first thirty minutes after her arrival, she just cried without control. Not knowing the reason for this teary performance, neither Sudhir nor Nandita were able to offer any consolation. Once she had felt better with the crying, she took stock of herself and just went on saying repeatedly that 'It was all my fault. I am responsible.'

Now, Sudhir and Nandita were able to get an idea of what was bothering Mridu. There was a lot of talk regarding Mridu's friendliness with one of the boys from the final year. A lot of it. Everyone was talking and appending to it as per their imaginative powers. The latest being that he had moved into her quarters. This was not true. The boy only visited her, now and then. As yet it had not reached the ears of the Principal. But this talk had to be dealt with. That was what Mridu was attempting to do.

'You remember him, don't you?' She asked Sudhir and Nandita. They both nodded. 'And you know what had happened, right?' The nods came again. 'So how am I wrong, now?' She wanted to know. The question was met with shrugs.

Arjun Chetia.

Anyone who saw Arjun Chetia in present times would refuse to believe that he was once a suave, young chap in the second year of his engineering course after having topped the highly competitive entrance examinations. He was the 'Everywhere, Everything' guy who had everybody's attention the moment he showed up. But that persona was now in hiding underneath an enlarged body mass and an overgrown crop of dense, perennially unkempt hair on the scalp and face.

This change had not come about dramatically. It had happened steadily. Technically, it had begun the day he had set his eyes on a young first year girl student during the Fresher's Party hosted by the seniors. The demure, petite thing did not as much even look at him and had barely managed to utter her name when he had asked her.

'Flying Fancies', Sudhir had warned him. After all, Sudhir was his student advisor. He felt it his responsibility to warn his ward of pitfalls. That did not deter Arjun. Cupid seemed to have been summoned out of the work hours and told to work overtime on this case. But either he was not putting his own heart into this matter or there was something seriously wrong with his arrows. For, even at the end of one year, he didn't seem to be making any significant progress at all. Neither was Arjun willing to give up.

Finding Cupid to be utterly useless, Arjun took matters into his own hands and marching upto her in the canteen one day, he went down on his knees and popped the question to her in full public view. The refusal also came in the same sphere of things. 'Is there someone else?' he had asked. Yes, she had confirmed.

If Cupid's arrows being useless was bad, then Cupid himself backfiring was much, much worse. In fact, a Cupid spurned college boy was a terrible being to have, the fellow having started to act strange. Arjun in particular had lost all sense of time and space, having taken to his bed and refused to have any connection with the world around him. He sought to transport himself from a world where there were a lot of emotions ranging from hunger to anger to a world where emotions had no importance at all.

Unfortunately, the only means of transportation available to this world involved a low grade of beverage that more often than not caused embarrassed drunken behavior; destruction of property, screaming and bawling mindlessly, being only a few of the characteristics of this behavior. Certainly, a respected educational institute like the ASEC could do without it and the ASEC decided to do without it by expelling Arjun. A lot happened after that.

First of all, he disappeared giving rise to rumours that ranged from having gone missing, drowned in the Brahmaputra- both willfully- to being kidnapped and then suspected to having joined the youth wing of the United Liberation Front of Assam, ULFA, the militant outfit. Though why the ULFA would want a youth wing when all of its leaders were young anyway, defied logic. But people had spoken and for now their words held.

Anyway, after having disappeared for two long years, he reappeared a changed man, showing up at Sudhir's home one late night. The change having been brought about at the annual Ambubachi mela, in Kamakhya Dham, that celebrates the Goddess' fertility. For days, he had lived and travelled with Hindu babas dressed in ragged loin clothes and rudraksh beads dangling around their necks to reach the Dham. The change enveloped him further as he stood in queue with a crowd of unruly devotees to eat the free khichuri distributed by the wealthy marwaris. That is when he decided that surely there had to be more to life than being a pointless wanderer robbed of romantic love.

Reaching Sudhir's familiar home, he was surprised at being recognized despite all the accumulated filth about his person. Sudhir, however, did not pester him about his whereabouts. Neither did Arjun ask anything about his family or anyone else from his past. Post a two day and three night long discussion, it was decided that the best course of action was, to complete his long pending education, first. Rest, could be thought of later.

Arjun's new beginning at IoTE as a final year student needed a lot of extra help. Sudhir alone would not be able to handle it. That is why he wrote to Mridu, then working for an MNC at NOIDA, if she would come over. She was unsure at first. After all, Arjun had categorically stated that he was ashamed to maintain relations with her and the family, after what had happened. 'But blood is thicker than water, isn't it?' Sudhir had reasoned.

As Arjun's elder sister, she knew it only too well. She agreed to join IoTE as a faculty member so that she could provide moral support towards Arjun's rehabilitation efforts. But first she would have to check with him, if he was willing to accept that support.

That is why she had invited him one evening to her quarters. Unfortunately, that discussion had obtained an uninvited audience from Dr. Hiramoni Nath and Dr. Madhobi Talukdar who had arrived to ask Mridu if she would like to join them for an evening walk- a most surprising invitation that by its very nature appeared to be spiked.

'Time to call their bluff!', said Nandita. 'There is no other way to it.'

44 THE END OF THE BEGININNG

Like every college, Ayote also had its own mechanism for dealing with undisciplined acts. It couldn't claim a good success rate but at crisis times, its existence did make a difference. So it was to exude this difference again that the Disciplinary Committee Meeting was called. The Committee compulsorily consisted of the Head of the various departments, the Hostel In Charge and those patrons of the Institute with a keen interest in the day to day welfare of the students. The Head of the Institution was also a part of the committee, but depending on the severity of the issue and his likelihood of getting irritated by the students concerned, he either took an active part or didn't.

In this case, he certainly was not going to participate actively. The boys and their misadventures had got on his nerves sufficiently to make him want to take a long sabbatical from office. He didn't want to change his image to that of one with a bee buzzing in the bonnet and there was every chance of this happening, if he came to the hearing. That explained his lack of interest in getting involved beyond leading the Committee's meeting.

He appointed one of the Heads of the Department to chair the Disciplinary Committee and deputed Sudhir to keep a strict watch on the proceedings while he himself just sat there as a passive spectator. Not that he didn't trust the Heads. They were fine. It was the representative from the hostel management that he had his doubts about. What with their haphazard thinking, it would not take time for yet another slapdash question to let disaster fill the place.

'So this is what you have been up to, huh?', asked The Chair. The two Ayotics did not have the option of disagreeing. So by default they agreed.

'Any defence?'
They shook their heads in the negative.

'In that case, the hearing is over. You may go now. The committee would declare its decision in the evening.'

The boys bowed out in silence. Minal Borthakur made an action that conveyed wanting to ask something. To this, the Head responded with a gesture that 'this case was done with'. That settled it.

'Hazarika to be sent in next!' ordered the Principal. 'Where does Hazarika fit in all this?', wondered The Chair of the Committee.

'Oh, you don't know?', asked the Principal thereafter going on to narrate how Hazarika had told the Thikedar's sidekicks about Rajib Deka's talent and his role in facilitating the meeting between the two which eventually had led to the success of the double dressing act. Of course, he had this information from Inspector Saikia who did a rather good job of interrogating the Thikedar to get the big picture of this incident.

The Thikedar had learnt of Rajib Deka's talents through Sarat his cashier who was a close friend of Hazarika's who had been the first person to tell Sarat about Rajib. Desperate to show off his skills, Rajib fell for the Thikedar's proposal with assistance from Tony. Tony's main interest in the plan was limited to finally getting to feel that his existence had a meaning by doing something out-of-the-box. And now, going by the state of things, it was going to cause Tony to experience being out-of-the-college as well. But he had accepted that life's like that and so he was okay with that.

Bikash Kumar's plan to kidnap the Thikedar's star money

earner was actually a boon in that, it revealed what these boys were doing. It was Bikash's misfortune that his ignorance about the current state of affairs in the world of village theatre had led him to capture the wrong person. Being Hazarika's cousin may or may not have had anything to do with it. But it certainly did not absolve Hazarika from being a suspect. He was reminded that he had been assigned this duty as a last chance to be a reformed employee of the Institute, whereupon failure would prove to be difficult for him.

Hazarika dutifully came in. Another one sided trial began and ended. It was a total no show. Hazarika never even got a chance to speak up. Perhaps it would be more correct to say that there was no need for him to talk. Because it seemed that the whole purpose of calling him before the Committee was to inform him that 'THIS WAS IT AND IT WAS ALL OVER'. What that translated in practice, they would be conveying to him later in the evening.

Sudhir told me that he had already conveyed what I had seen of the boys to the Committee and so I might be spared from having to make an appearance at the hearing, something which would have unnecessarily invited sensationalism. I was glad of it. For I certainly did not have any intentions of leaving behind this kind of a teaching footprint during my short stint, however minor it may have been. So like everyone else, I awaited the results of the proceedings to be declared in the evening.

Evening saw a sizeable crowd assembled in front of the notice board. Everyone was reading the decision of the Disciplinary Committee.

NOTICE TO FACULTY, STUDENTS & STAFF

This is to inform that the Disciplinary Committee has decided to suspend the following students for the rest of the semester:

1. Rajib Deka   First Semester   ME

2. Antony Asoke Baruah   Third Semester   ME

It came to the notice to the Committee that the above mentioned students violated hostel rules and college discipline thereby bringing in a lot of disrepute to themselves, their parents and this Institution.

Students not having academic interest should enroll in other colleges and not here as it disturbs the scholarly environment of the Institute.

Further, please note that the following staff member who was under suspension during the Tony Baruah Missing case has now been sacked from position:

1.   Bipin Hazarika

This person should not be encouraged by anyone, anywhere near the institute.

Head

        Institute of Technical Education, Imranpur

Head of Administration

        Institute of Technical Education, Imranpur

In Charge, Hostel Operations

        Institute of Technical Education, Imranpur

45 CARRYING ON

By the time all the formalities with the expulsions had been carried out, it was once again exam time at IoTE. This time, for a record, all the faculty members across the departments signed up for invigilation duties. Simply because it gave them the opportunity to discuss and dissect the episode to the minutest details without feeling guilty of neglecting their duties and they did all of that over plates of snacks and tea that came free with the invigilating duty.

'I just can't believe it!' Exclaimed the chemistry teacher throwing her hands up in the air to emphasis the point. 'I could never even dream of such a thing.' But then going by her experiences, there were several things she was capable of dreaming. Like, a student being unable to differentiate between a test tube and a beaker despite twelve years of rigorous schooling. Or the most recent instance of being rebuked by a much younger colleague for suspecting her brother to be, instead 'the other party' in her relationship with her fiancé. It embarrassed the chemistry teacher massively. Worse, when she tried to share it with the maths teacher, she claimed to be unwell and refused to talk to her. Eventually, she severed all relations as well. A very divisive collaboration, it was widely acknowledged.

'Can you?' She asked me. It wasn't clear to me if she was asking of my ability to believe or dream. I would have rather preferred the latter, though. It would have been easy to answer. After all I had dreamt of a lot of weird things. One more would not have made a difference. Beliefs and believing was altogether different.

More so in this case, because I was actually at the scene.

'You were?' She asked totally bewildered. The last time she felt this level of bewilderment was when she realized I had two fathers. Seemed to me that, she had a long list of things she could not believe in and be bewildered about. It was definitely not the thing that her foreign degree had prepared her for. However, at that moment, more important that her power of believing was my presence in that rare climax scene of a police chase that seldom came in the dreams and beliefs of assistant professors. She wanted the details. In other words, I was going to have to provide the freshest fodders for gossip.

This whole incident of the boys shape-shifting appeared ridiculous to me. Yet, I was not going to be spared until they had heard my narration of the chain of events. Not even Ph.D holders and ex IIT professors.

It was not always that they had students providing such exciting misadventures. It was unprecedented in the history of the Institute. And given the historic decision taken by the disciplinary committee so early in the history of the Institute, it was not likely to repeat itself in the future any time sooner. So naturally the campus had a right to regale itself with tales about this. In course of things, pretty much had been lost track of and it was obvious that it would take some time for the Institute to settle back to its old rhythm.

Everyone had their own sources of getting the details. If the faculty got to hear of it first from the Head of the Institute and the disciplinary committee over cups of tea in the Principal's Office, then they later sought and received deeper insights from Sudhir and occasionally from me at the Dr B. N Saikia Lab with the tea-lady also joining to contribute her fair share.

The entire students community got to hear it from the fallen heroes Tony and Rajib themselves in the canteen over plates of badly cooked egg noodles with burnt cabbage- a meal that never failed to make them wonder at the cooking sensibilities and menu choices of the Hostel Management. From their point of view, the decision was totally unexpected even though they had read about DISciplinary

COmmittees in an immensely popular book on the lives of mischief makers at the IIT. Though, when it came to the DISCO of their own college, they had chosen to sing 'Disco Dancer' every time a professor brought it to their notice. But now they were eating their own words along with the badly cooked egg noodles with burnt cabbage as side dish.

If this left a bad taste in their mouths, it left a hole in Tony's heart when he saw Gitusmita pass by him, walking along with The King, elbows locked. As they came close to him, The King slapped a hand on his back saying 'Hard luck, man!' and that 'you'll be back and rocking soon, bro!' while she merely cocked her head away and then, squeezing the arm of The King, got him to walk away from there with her.

Meanwhile, the support staff and security had to rely on whatever information was provided by their supervisors. They could not seek it on their own as they had officially excommunicated Hazarika. Though, the occasional defaulter did exchange a word or two with him and so in bits and pieces his side of the story also managed to trickle in.

I was myself quite amused to be at the center of the chase and I agree it provided much entertainment. I was thoroughly entertained, no doubt. But that was just about it. I didn't want to add fictionalized tit bits to it for more entertainment and that too for others.

Except for collaborating on whatever others had heard from Sudhir, I kept largely to myself. Most surprisingly, rather than being left alone, I found myself being a dumping bag for any latest news anybody heard. I was told these things not because they felt it their duty to keep me updated. It was because they felt they had to get rid of these things and what better way than to tell me- somebody with whom it would remain safe. They would always end up telling me, 'you didn't hear it from me, okay?' and I would oblige them with an 'okay'.

Anyway, I was busy, not just with the college work but in the free time too, trying to put together a Border War Veterans'

Association. I was convinced that just as I was a wonderful story that the war had produced, it was quite likely that there would be other stories also that were equally interesting. I had first bounced this idea to koka. His response was that there was already an annual War Memorial Prayer Meet where people met and prayed. Though koka himself no longer went since he was now the sole surviving member of his generation and that made him feel very ghostly when he showed up.

'These young chaps go, but', he said, meaning of course his grand sons for whom it still had a huge meaning. After all, they were now the only family in the village that had the only 'Burra Dagoria' who fought many an illustrious battle.

I then talked it out with Dinesh Barua. He was very forthcoming of the idea. In fact he had sent me a packet full of photos associated with the war hoping that I could learn more from them. They were copies of the originals he had in his possession. He felt that all of these stories had spent enough time locked up in a drawer and should now be let out. If that happened to be a common, easy to access platform, so much the better. To me that meant an online community. Aha!

While the rest of the college busied itself on their terms, I made some significant decisions now that my search for the elusive Mr. Bharadwaj was over. It was in this regard that I wanted to have a word with the Head, now that things were working back in place.

'Sir?' I opened the conversation directly. Exchange of pleasantries rarely made an impression on this man.

'Yes?'

'I wanted to apply for a week's leave, sir.'

'Why?'

'Need to go to the War Cemetery, sir.'

Fear gripped the man as he looked at me upon hearing this.

Once in the past he had caught me reading about war memorials in the north east when he had come searching for Sudhir in the Dr B. N Saikia Lab. Then, twice in the past he had caught me looking up various graves on different websites as part of the grave spotting exercise a citizen's welfare agency had initiated in order to connect survivors of dead soldiers in various battles with their descendants. I had myself enrolled in this in the hope of making a breakthrough on my search.

All this while, he had never questioned my intentions. Now, learning about my intention to visit them, frightful thoughts were stirring up in his mind. I could sense that. After an episode of Houdini Trick by the boys, kidnapping of fake actors and missing people, he could surely do without an assistant professor who exorcises ghosts. I understood.

'It is about the real Mr. Bharadwaj.'

I was not sure if that made things clear for him. To me it certainly did not look like he had. I thought maybe I should clarify that it was about my 'original' father. But then I remembered that he had had enough of originals and duplicities. I should not be adding more to it. I put it in a manner that gave sufficient hints on the nature of how this 'Mr. Bharadwaj' affected my existence and therefore my relationship with him.

'Ah, ok, sure. You may leave. Granted, granted.' He was relieved. The response seemed more like wanting to get rid of me. 'Ashima', he called out just as I reached the door.

'Sir?'

'One minute. Come here.'

'Yes, sir?'

I walked back to his desk.

'You know who I am?' He asked.

I was floored by the question. It was all together a very abrupt and an awkward question to ask. Why me, all of us knew who he was! I told him that. 'No.. no..', he protested. 'as in…'

'Your name?' I suggested, having managed to spy on his name plate his complete credentials. It said Dr. Nabajyoti Goswami, Ph.D.

'No, no', he said again, getting distressed that he wasn't getting the right words to say. I also didn't know what to say. It is always most puzzling when words vanish when needed the most. Finally, after a confused pause he said 'I know you' which was also not exactly an earth shattering discovery to make since as the Head of the Institution he was supposed to know who I was.

'I know you', he insisted again suggesting that somehow I knew what he was trying to convey. But I didn't and to save the situation from developing into one where he may start shouting, I said, 'Sorry?' The Head was now desperate to get out with what he had intended to say.

'My brother is Captain Nayanjyoti Goswami.' He said. That sounded pretty cool to me until he completed the sentence saying 'but people know him as Captain Bharadwaj Bordoloi. He took after the name we called him by at home.'

'Wh-' My jaws dropped and I think it remained like that for a full one minute before I exclaimed, 'You are my uncle!' when I had regained some composure. 'See, you know me', he pointed out. 'And I know you too.'

For the next few minutes, I looked at him in bewilderment. And then it struck me that by claiming to 'know' what he was trying to say is that he and I were related. But 'related' is the last word that would come to the mind of an Uncle upon meeting his long lost, seldom seen, never cared for, and forbidden by family, niece even if he was a man of strong academic credentials.

'But--'

'Sarah told me. She didn't want you to know. She thought it is best the way it is. But I thought ….It's the least we can do for you now.'

It was no deceased Uncle that had written to me that first letter. It was him. My Aunt Sarah had happened to meet the family during one of the annual war memorial prayer meets. She had contemplated telling them about me and about a letter by her brother stating the hidden truth, should such a development choose to happen but refrained many times before finally talking it out. The Brendon family had decided that the matter was closed. There was no need to mention about it to anyone. Aunt herself had championed this thought. But it hit her from inside that if I was actually born of a hero, I should know that and that, I didn't.

This finally prompted her to make up her mind to meet Dr. Nabajyoti Goswami and through the letters, both the families came clean on this.

'I would have told you myself but then Sarah told me you were already finding things out. And then when I saw it in the papers, I asked Dinesh if he could help.'

'Dinesh Barua? You know him?'

The newly discovered uncle nodded.

'Our father owned a tea estate too. But it was too much for him to take care of it. So he sold it off to Dinesh's father'. He had then gone on to do other business that caused less threat to life. And of his children, while Naba went ahead to do academics, Nayan, my father took up the cause of fighting the enemy. Suddenly the word 'diversify' popped up in my head.

'Your father was a good man.' he said.

'Which one?' I asked and instantly regretted.

The uncle also sensed it and to me it seemed like he too was regretting having made that statement. From what I had gathered, they must have had quite a turbulent time coming to terms with the junior Bharadwaj's off the battlefield antics. After much consideration he said, 'Both', before hastily adding that 'James Brendon was a great man'. I agreed on that. For, he was after all a rather 'cool' daddy to have. 'I should leave now.' I said. 'Yes.' And on that note, I bowed my head and stretched down to touch his feet. I was not sure if there was something I could do beyond that.

'Sir?'

'Yes?'

'Can I just be Ashima?'

'What are you just now?'

'Ashima B. Brendon'

'Ah!!'

He understood. He always had known it from the unexpanded 'B' in my name. 'How about Ashima Brendwaj?' He offered after thinking for a minute. It sounded like the murderous cousin of Brainwash, only badly mispronounced.

'Bhardon?'

'Sir?'

'Ah, joking!!'

'It is ok, sir. Thanks for the help.'

With that, I walked out of the room.

When I returned to my quarters to start packing, my eyes fell on the packet of photos that Dinesh Barua had sent me. I had only given them a cursory glance. But now, going through them one by one in detail, I was feeling very proud to possess such historic photos. One of them, I noticed was that of the graves at the War Cemetery. On looking closer I realized it was Captain Bharadwaj's grave. On the plaque, it was written,

'Sleep Tight, daddy!

Capt. Nayanjyoti Goswami, 1955-1985

KIA, Merapani Border War.

This memorial was erected by his widow and infant daughter'

I had never known my father and it was equally likely that he too never knew about my existence. But here I was bidding him adieu every single night. Behind the photo, Dinesh Barua had scribbled that it was actually my other father- Daddy Brendon who had commissioned this in secrecy and used to visit this war hero in the cemetery every year, until he died. He had found that out from the register at the cemetery.

With that, I made up my mind.

I was not going to be bothered about my name anymore. I would make one of my own. For now, 'Ashima Bharadwaj- Brendon' was good enough. And if I met that big bad bullying boy from my school days, I would tell him that as well.

I made a call to my Aunt and told her that not only did I find my missing 'B' father, but that I met his brother as well and that I now know the whos and whys and hows of that letter which I received. She sounded a little concerned when I mentioned the brother. 'Ah, well, he was nervous', I admitted to her. 'But we are all cool now.' I assured her.

I could sense her relief and the tears at work too. I then told her about my planned journey. To my disappointment, her first response was a mere 'Oh!', followed by silence. I didn't understand this, until after an elaborate pause she asked, 'So then when can Varun come to meet you?'

So Mr. Horoscope had experienced a change of planetary alignments, huh?

'I don't know.' I replied, sounding quite dismissive about it. I really didn't and for some reason I didn't seem excited about him anymore.

I didn't want to keep relations with people who showed up and vanished as per their convenience. Aunt wished me a safe journey and ordered me to land straight at her place once I was back. 'Else-', I knew what that threat meant.

Later that evening, picking up my bags, I left for my journey towards the borders and the Lake of No Return, wishing IoTE the best for the next coming days. If IoTE had anything more to do with this business of boys getting lost and mixed up in connection with Rubul Kalita, then, it surely was going to be another story to tell, upon my return from the borders. Meanwhile, Inspector Saikia was busy gathering clues as to what led to his disappearance.

ABOUT THE AUTHOR

Ambalika is a lazy writer and full time dreamer constantly fantasizing about life in outer space. She is exceptionally talented in hitting people with surprises, owing to some leftover karma from a past life lived as a meteoroid. A firm believer that life is best spent sky gazing, living off kebabs and watching kites fly, she made her writing debut with 'You Adored, Me Ignored'. She is also the author of 'The Joy of Being Jay'.